The last Blue Planet

Earth in 2099 and the quest for space habitats

DM Ole Kiminta

The last blue planet

DM Ole Kiminta

Published by KBros, 2025.

THE LAST BLUE PLANET

First edition. April 25, 2025.

Copyright © 2025 DM Ole Kiminta.

ISBN: 978-1069323194

Written by DM Ole Kiminta.

Also by DM Ole Kiminta

How the Western Democracies failed the world
Supporting Refugees in their Homelands
Dissuading Global War Mongers:
Dissuading war mongers
La Libération Monétaire en Afrique
Canada Post: Management failure to modernise mail systems
Canada Post management failure to modernise mail systems
Canada Post: Management failure to modernise mail systems
Live to be 200
Aim to live for 200
Aim to live to be 200
Western democracies failed the world economies
Wrong foot forward: US-Canada trade wars
Canada begs to differ: Never a 51st state of USA
Tethered to the Kitchen
Nous ne pouvons pas être le 51e État des États-Unis
Nous ne serons jamais le 51ème état des États-Unis.
The Nephilim and the erosion of moral boundaries
Every human is an advocate for World Peace
The diplomatic dilemma of Western Sahara
Every human: Advocate for World Peace
The last blue planet

Table of Contents

Chapter 1: The State of Earth in 2099

When humans have exhausted everything

The human race on this planet has worried repeatedly about the end of the world, the religious promises of a heaven and if you are a scientist, you worry night and day about an approaching giant asteroid hitting the earth and moving it to a wrong orbit and changing climate for ever. others who study everything about our planet worry about humans exhausting everything, others might skive the whole idea of the sun dying one day and just live and not give a flake in hell about the environment. We cannot assume that if by a stroke of luck, the earthlings can find a hostable planet with advanced civilisation and will therefore be permissible just to fly in and settle, no, just as we may be sympathetic to host a race of non-earthlings as planetary refugees and throw out others, it is likely that the only Scott-free entry is if we find a non-occupied habitable planet out there. So, what happens to our descendants if they don't start turning every stone bottom-side up in a hurry to find something a century from now (2025) or just half of it, let's say 2099?

Let us assume that it is now year 2099 and the earth has changed because of many things including foolish human greed and endless wars, what then?

Book Overview

The first part of this book has narrated an ambitious move by the earthlings beyond year 2099 and what would have happened to the planet earth with all the hullabaloos of climate change etc. On the second part of the book, I have tried to avail a situation that assumes that we start from "now" (year 2025) and progress to year 2099. In other words, what happens or what we do between now and year 2099. So, we start with the first part of the book with the notion that it is now year 2099 and what has happened to the planet.

Environmental challenges in 2099 have reached unprecedented levels, shaping the landscape of both Earth and the future of space exploration. The effects of climate change, habitat destruction, and pollution have intensified, prompting urgent discussions about the sustainability of life on our planet. Rising sea levels have submerged coastal cities, while extreme weather events have become commonplace, disrupting ecosystems and human settlements alike. In this context, the quest for space habitats has gained momentum, as humanity seeks alternatives to a deteriorating Earth. Can you see this predicament confronting the human race on these few lines you just read? It is an emergency that should have been prevented so long ago when the humans were burning fossil fuel and other polluting substances and saying no to those nations and individuals including scientists who were in the forefront of conveying the ominous depletion of ozone layer and other changes could have been prevented (assuming we are now in 2099).

One of the most pressing issues is the depletion of natural resources, driven by an ever-growing global population and unsustainable consumption patterns. Freshwater scarcity affects billions, while deforestation continues to threaten biodiversity. The demand for energy has led to a surge in renewable energy technologies, focusing on solar, wind, and geothermal sources. Technological innovations are essential for transitioning to a sustainable energy model, but they also present challenges, such as the environmental impact of manufacturing and disposing of solar panels and batteries.

Artificial intelligence has emerged as a crucial tool in addressing environmental challenges. AI systems are now deployed for real-time environmental monitoring, enabling precise data collection on air and water quality, wildlife populations, and deforestation rates. These advancements allow for quicker responses to ecological crises and foster more effective conservation strategies. However, the reliance on AI raises questions about reliance on technology and the need for ethical considerations in its application, particularly in vulnerable ecosystems.

As urban areas grapple with the consequences of environmental degradation, cities in 2099 are focusing on sustainability. Innovations in urban planning and green architecture are aimed at creating self-sustaining environments. Vertical gardens, green roofs, and urban forests are becoming integral components of city landscapes, improving air quality and providing habitats for wildlife. These initiatives serve as models for potential colonisation efforts beyond Earth, highlighting the importance of integrating ecological principles into future habitats.

The intersection of environmental challenges and space exploration presents both opportunities and risks. The drive to establish colonies on other planets is fuelled by the need to ensure humanity's survival. However, this ambition must be tempered with a commitment to preserving earth's ecosystems. The lessons learned from managing our planet's resources will inform how we approach extraterrestrial colonisation. As we look to the stars, the importance of responsible stewardship of both earth and potential new worlds cannot be overstated, ensuring that we do not repeat the mistakes of the past.

Socioeconomic impacts

In 2099, the socioeconomic landscape of Earth has been profoundly altered by the ongoing challenges of climate change, resource scarcity, and the pursuit of space exploration. As humanity grapples with the consequences of environmental degradation, the socioeconomic impacts are evident in every facet of life. Innovative technologies aimed at sustainable living have become essential, shaping new economies and altering traditional job markets. The transition to renewable energy has not only created employment opportunities in sectors such as solar, wind, and bioenergy but has also led to the emergence of new industries focused on energy efficiency and environmental monitoring.

The quest for space habitats has driven significant investment in research and development, resulting in breakthroughs that have ripple effects on earth's economy. Companies focused on space colonisation have generated demand for advanced materials and technologies, which in turn stimulates local economies. The collaboration between public sectors and private enterprises has facilitated the creation of jobs in engineering, robotics, and artificial intelligence, fostering a workforce adept at navigating the complexities of both terrestrial and extraterrestrial environments. This convergence of interests has led to a more dynamic economic landscape, characterised by a blend of traditional industries and cutting-edge technology.

However, the drive towards space exploration and technological innovation has also exacerbated socioeconomic disparities. While urban centres thrive with new opportunities, rural areas often struggle to keep pace with rapid advancements. The digital divide remains a pressing issue, as access to technology and education is unevenly distributed. Policies aimed at promoting equity and inclusion are crucial to ensure that all communities can benefit from the advancements in renewable energy and AI. Without intentional efforts to bridge these gaps, the socioeconomic divide could widen, leading to increased social tensions and economic instability.

Environmental monitoring, powered by artificial intelligence, has transformed how societies manage resources and respond to ecological challenges. With real-time data collection and analysis, communities are better equipped to address issues such as pollution, deforestation, and biodiversity loss. This proactive approach not only enhances environmental stewardship but also leads to more informed economic decisions. As businesses and governments rely on accurate environmental data, industries are increasingly held accountable for their impact on ecosystems, prompting a shift towards sustainable practices that align economic growth with environmental health.

In this era of transformation, the interplay between socioeconomic factors and technological advancements will shape the future of Earth and its inhabitants. The pursuit of space habitats reflects humanity's resilience and adaptability, but it also serves as a reminder of the importance of addressing the challenges faced on our home planet. As we venture beyond Earth, the lessons learned from socioeconomic impacts will inform our strategies for sustainable living and cooperation, ensuring that the next chapter in our journey is marked by inclusivity, innovation, and a commitment to preserving the delicate balance of our planet.

Technological Advancements

In 2099, technological advancements have dramatically reshaped the landscape of Earth and the possibilities beyond it. The challenges posed by climate change, resource depletion, and overpopulation have spurred innovation in various fields. One of the most significant developments has been in renewable energy technologies. Solar panels, wind turbines, and bioenergy systems have become more efficient and affordable, allowing for a transition away from fossil fuels. The integration of smart grids has enabled real-time energy distribution, optimising energy consumption and reducing waste. These advancements not only help mitigate environmental impacts but also empower communities to harness local resources for sustainable living.

Artificial intelligence has emerged as a transformative force in environmental monitoring and management. In 2099, AI systems are employed to track climate patterns, predict natural disasters, and monitor biodiversity. These systems analyse vast amounts of data from satellites, drones, and ground sensors, providing insights that were previously unattainable. Machine learning algorithms can identify trends and anomalies in ecosystems, enabling more proactive and effective responses to environmental challenges. This level of monitoring has facilitated better resource management and has helped in the restoration of ecosystems that were once thought to be irreparably damaged.

Space exploration has been significantly enhanced by technological innovations, allowing humanity to extend its reach beyond Earth. Advances in propulsion systems, such as ion thrusters and nuclear thermal engines, have reduced travel time to other planets and asteroids. The development of autonomous spacecraft equipped with AI has revolutionized missions, allowing for real-time decision-making in the harsh environments of space. These technologies not only increase the feasibility of crewed missions to Mars (or others discovered by 2099) and beyond but also pave the way for the establishment of outposts and research stations on other celestial bodies, marking the beginning of a new era in human exploration.

The quest for space habitats has also benefited from innovations in materials science and robotics. In 2099, engineers utilise advanced composites and 3D printing technologies to construct habitats that can withstand the rigors of space and support human life. Robotic systems play a crucial role in the construction and maintenance of these habitats, enabling the assembly of structures on the Moon and Mars using local resources. This approach reduces the need to transport materials from Earth, making the colonisation of other planets more sustainable and cost-effective. The successful establishment of space habitats is a pivotal step toward ensuring humanity's survival beyond Earth.

As technology continues to evolve, the integration of these advancements will play a crucial role in shaping a sustainable future both on Earth and in space. The collaboration between various fields, including renewable energy, artificial intelligence, and aerospace engineering, fosters a holistic approach to solving global challenges. The innovations of 2099 not only reflect humanity's ingenuity but also emphasise the importance of responsible stewardship of our planet and the cosmos. This synergy between technology and environmental consciousness is essential as we embark on the next chapter of human existence, navigating the delicate balance between exploration and preservation.

Chapter 2: The rise of space exploration

The year 2099 represents a pivotal moment in human history, shaped by centuries of exploration, technological advancements, and environmental challenges. The narrative of space exploration began in the mid-20th century when humanity first ventured beyond Earth's atmosphere. The Space Age, marked by the launch of Sputnik in 1957, ignited a global fascination with the cosmos and set the stage for future endeavours. By the late 20th century, technological innovations had significantly advanced, enabling more sophisticated space missions and fostering an international collaborative spirit. This foundation laid the groundwork for the ambitious plans to colonise other celestial bodies, particularly as Earth faced increasing environmental degradation.

As the 21st century unfolded, the effects of climate change became increasingly evident. Rising sea levels, extreme weather events, and loss of biodiversity prompted urgent calls for sustainable practices and renewable energy solutions. Nations around the world recognised the need for a unified approach to environmental protection, leading to international agreements aimed at reducing carbon emissions and promoting green technologies. The urgency of these issues acted as a catalyst for innovation, resulting in breakthroughs in solar, wind, and other renewable energy sources. By 2099, these innovations were not only essential for Earth's survival but also provided the energy needed for expanding space exploration efforts.

The concept of utilising space habitats emerged as a feasible solution to Earth's challenges. With the development of advanced technologies, including artificial intelligence and robotics, humanity began to envision self-sustaining colonies beyond Earth. These habitats would serve as a refuge for those seeking to escape the deteriorating conditions on earth, as well as a testing ground for new technologies. The exploration of Mars and other celestial bodies became a focal point for scientific research and investment, driven by the belief that extraterrestrial environments could support human life with the right technological enhancements.

The role of artificial intelligence in monitoring environmental conditions on earth and beyond cannot be overstated. By 2099, AI systems had evolved to manage vast amounts of data collected from satellites and sensors, enabling real-time analysis of climate patterns and resource availability. This technology played a crucial role in optimising energy consumption, improving agricultural practices, and ensuring sustainable resource management on earth. Additionally, AI supported the development of space habitats by facilitating autonomous systems that could maintain life-supporting environments, thus reducing the need for constant human oversight.

The historical context of 2099 is not merely a reflection of technological progress but also of humanity's resilience and adaptability. The journey from Earth to the stars has been fraught with challenges, yet it has also been a testament to human ingenuity. As society has navigated the complexities of environmental crises and explored the vastness of space, the lessons learned have underscored the importance of sustainable practices and the need for a harmonious relationship with both our planet and the universe. This intricate tapestry of history informs the ongoing quest for space habitats, shaping the future of humanity as we strive to secure a viable existence beyond Earth.

Key Players in Space Exploration

The realm of space exploration in 2099 is shaped by a diverse array of key players, each contributing unique resources, expertise, and vision to the quest for sustainable habitats beyond Earth. National space agencies, such as NASA, ESA, and CNSA, remain at the forefront of exploration, driving advancements in technology and international cooperation. These organisations not only conduct groundbreaking missions to the Moon and Mars but also focus on developing the infrastructure needed for human habitation in space. Their commitment to research and development is critical, as they work to overcome the challenges posed by long-duration spaceflight and the harsh conditions of extraterrestrial environments.

In addition to government entities, private companies have emerged as vital contributors to space exploration. Firms like SpaceX, Blue Origin, and Virgin Galactic have revolutionised access to space through innovative launch systems and reusable rocket technology. Their relentless pursuit of cost-effective solutions has significantly lowered the barriers to entry for space missions. As these companies expand their capabilities, they are also investing in developing space habitats, mining operations on asteroids, and in-situ resource utilisation techniques that could support human life on other celestial bodies. The collaboration between public and private sectors fosters a dynamic ecosystem that accelerates technological advancements and broadens the possibilities for colonisation.

Academic institutions and research organisations play a significant role in advancing knowledge and technology related to space exploration. Universities worldwide conduct essential research on areas such as astrobiology, planetary science, and environmental monitoring, contributing to the understanding of life-support systems for future habitats. Interdisciplinary collaboration among scientists, engineers, and environmental experts is crucial for devising sustainable solutions that can be implemented in extraterrestrial environments. These institutions also train the next generation of space explorers, ensuring that the workforce is equipped with the necessary skills to tackle future challenges.

Artificial intelligence (AI) has become an indispensable tool in the field of space exploration. AI systems are employed to analyse vast amounts of data collected from space missions, enhancing decision-making processes and enabling autonomous operations in remote environments. Machine learning algorithms assist in optimising resource management, monitoring environmental conditions, and predicting potential hazards in space habitats. As AI continues to evolve, its integration into space exploration initiatives will facilitate safer and more efficient missions, ultimately enhancing our ability to establish sustainable colonies beyond Earth.

Lastly, international collaboration is a crucial element in the future of space exploration. As nations recognise the shared challenges of expanding into space, partnerships are being forged to combine expertise and resources. Initiatives such as the Artemis program and the Lunar Gateway project exemplify how countries can work together to create a sustainable presence on the Moon and beyond. These collaborative efforts not only promote peaceful use of outer space but also foster innovation and knowledge sharing that can benefit all of humanity. As we move toward a future where space habitats may become a reality, the synergy among these key players will be fundamental in shaping our journey into the cosmos.

Milestones Achieved

In 2099, humanity reached significant milestones in its journey towards sustainable living on Earth and the exploration of space habitats. The convergence of technological innovations and a collective commitment to environmental stewardship allowed society to overcome challenges that once seemed insurmountable. These achievements not only transformed life on Earth but also laid the groundwork for humanity's expansion beyond its home planet.

One of the most notable milestones was the successful implementation of global renewable energy systems. By harnessing solar, wind, ocean, and geothermal resources, nations transitioned away from fossil fuels, leading to a dramatic reduction in greenhouse gas emissions. The development of advanced energy storage technologies enabled the efficient capture and use of renewable energy, ensuring a stable power supply even during periods of low generation. This shift not only mitigated climate change but also stimulated economic growth, with millions of jobs created in the green technology sector.

In parallel to advancements in renewable energy, artificial intelligence emerged as a pivotal tool in environmental monitoring and management. AI systems were deployed to analyse vast amounts of ecological data, allowing for precise tracking of biodiversity and ecosystem health. These systems provided insights that guided conservation efforts, helping to protect endangered species and restore damaged habitats. Moreover, AI-driven predictive models enabled governments and organisations to make informed decisions about land use and resource allocation, fostering a more sustainable relationship with nature.

Humanity's ambition to explore space saw remarkable progress, with the establishment of permanent colonies on the Moon and Mars. These habitats served as testing grounds for sustainable living in extraterrestrial environments, utilising in-situ resources to support life. Innovations in life support systems, including closed-loop ecological systems and waste recycling technologies, were crucial in making these colonies viable. The knowledge gained from these endeavours not only advanced space exploration but also inspired new practices on Earth, further reinforcing the planet's resilience.

The collaboration between governments, private enterprises, and international organisations marked another major milestone in this era. A global framework for space exploration emerged, emphasising cooperation over competition. This collaborative spirit facilitated knowledge sharing, resource pooling, and joint missions, accelerating progress in both space colonisation and environmental restoration on Earth. As a result, humanity entered a new era defined by shared goals, where the quest for survival on a blue planet and the exploration of the cosmos went hand in hand, paving the way for a sustainable future for generations to come.

Chapter 3: The Quest for Space Habitats
Identifying Suitable Celestial Bodies

Identifying suitable celestial bodies for human habitation is a critical step in the quest for space habitats, particularly as Earth faces increasing environmental challenges in 2099. As the impacts of climate change and resource depletion intensify, the search for alternatives beyond our home planet has become more urgent.

Scientists and researchers are now focusing on a range of celestial bodies, including moons, asteroids, and planets within our solar system, that may offer the necessary conditions for human life or could be transformed into habitable environments through technological innovations.

One of the primary candidates for colonization is Mars, due to its relative proximity and similarities to Earth. While the Martian atmosphere is thin and composed mainly of carbon dioxide, advancements in terraforming technologies could potentially alter its environment to support human life. Recent studies have indicated that subsurface water ice exists on Mars, which could be a vital resource for future colonists. Furthermore, the planet's day length is similar to Earth's, providing a familiar rhythm for human activities. The ongoing exploration missions are critical in gathering data on its geology and climate, which will inform future habitat designs.

The moons of Jupiter and Saturn are also gaining attention as potential habitats. Europa, one of Jupiter's moons, is believed to harbor a vast ocean beneath its icy crust, making it a prime candidate for astrobiological studies. If life exists in such extreme conditions, it may provide insights into the resilience of life forms and potential adaptations for human survival. Similarly, Titan, Saturn's largest moon, features a dense atmosphere and surface lakes of liquid methane and ethane. These unique characteristics present opportunities for innovative energy solutions and resource extraction that could support human habitats.

Asteroids represent another intriguing avenue for exploration and colonization. These celestial bodies are abundant in valuable minerals and could serve as stepping stones for deeper space missions. The advancement of artificial intelligence in environmental monitoring and resource management could enable efficient mining operations on asteroids, providing not only materials for construction but also oxygen and water for sustaining human life. By developing technologies to extract and utilize these resources, humanity could create a sustainable presence in space, reducing the reliance on Earth's dwindling supplies.

As we venture beyond Earth, careful consideration must be given to the long-term implications of colonizing other celestial bodies. Ethical frameworks will need to be established to address issues such as planetary protection and the potential consequences of altering extraterrestrial environments. The integration of AI in monitoring these environments will be crucial in ensuring that human activities do not cause irreversible harm. By identifying suitable celestial bodies and developing technologies to support human life, we can not only secure a future for humanity in space but also foster a deeper understanding of our place in the universe.

Designing Sustainable Habitats

Designing sustainable habitats has become an imperative focus as humanity navigates the challenges posed by climate change and dwindling natural resources. In the year 2099, these habitats must not only support human life but also integrate seamlessly with the surrounding environment. This requires a multidisciplinary approach that combines architecture, ecology, and technology to create spaces that are energy-efficient, resilient, and capable of adapting to the changing climate. By prioritizing sustainability, future habitats can minimize their ecological footprint and promote biodiversity, ensuring a healthier planet for both current and future generations.

Innovative architectural designs play a crucial role in the development of sustainable habitats. In 2099, buildings are increasingly constructed using biomimicry, which draws inspiration from nature's designs and processes. Structures that resemble natural forms can enhance energy efficiency and reduce resource consumption. For instance, buildings designed to mimic termite mounds maintain constant internal temperatures without the need for conventional heating or cooling systems. The integration of living walls and green roofs not only improves air quality but also provides insulation, further reducing energy demands. Such designs demonstrate how closely aligning human structures with natural systems can yield significant environmental benefits.

Renewable energy technologies are at the forefront of sustainable habitat design. In the quest for energy independence, habitats in 2099 are equipped with advanced solar panels, wind turbines, and geothermal systems. These technologies harness renewable resources to provide clean energy, thus eliminating reliance on fossil fuels. More importantly, the advent of energy-storage solutions allows habitats to maintain a consistent energy supply, even during periods of low production. As energy efficiency continues to improve, the incorporation of smart grids powered by artificial intelligence enables real-time monitoring and management of energy use, optimizing consumption and minimizing waste.

Artificial intelligence plays a transformative role in environmental monitoring within sustainable habitats. In 2099, AI systems are employed to assess and manage the health of ecosystems surrounding human settlements. These systems can detect changes in environmental conditions, such as temperature fluctuations, air quality, and water availability, allowing for timely interventions to mitigate adverse impacts. Furthermore, AI can enhance sustainability by optimizing resource management, such as water and waste recycling, ensuring that these habitats maintain a balance with their natural surroundings. This intelligent monitoring not only supports human habitation but also fosters the recovery and preservation of local ecosystems.

The design of sustainable habitats in 2099 reflects a paradigm shift in how humanity interacts with the Earth. By embracing innovative architectural practices, renewable energy technologies, and advanced monitoring systems, future habitats can thrive while protecting the planet. The integration of these elements creates a harmonious living environment that prioritizes both human well-being and ecological health. As we move forward into an era of space exploration and colonization, the lessons learned from designing sustainable habitats on Earth will serve as a foundation for creating viable living spaces beyond our home planet, ensuring that humanity can thrive in harmony with the universe.

Challenges of Space Living

Living in space presents a unique set of challenges that differ significantly from those encountered on Earth. The absence of a breathable atmosphere, extreme temperatures, and the vacuum of space create an environment that requires innovative solutions for human survival. In 2099, as humanity endeavors to establish permanent habitats beyond Earth, addressing these challenges is paramount. The development of efficient life-support systems, advanced materials for construction, and sustainable energy sources are critical for ensuring the safety and well-being of space residents.

One of the primary challenges of space living is the need for a reliable source of breathable air. In a closed environment, such as a space habitat, carbon dioxide levels can rise rapidly due to human respiration and other processes. Technologies such as advanced biological systems, which use algae or plants to convert carbon dioxide back into oxygen, are being explored. Additionally, systems that recycle air by removing impurities are essential. By 2099, innovations in artificial photosynthesis and bioregenerative life support systems may provide efficient solutions for maintaining air quality in space.

Radiation exposure poses another significant risk to inhabitants of space habitats. Unlike Earth, which is protected by its magnetic field and atmosphere, space exposes individuals to harmful cosmic rays and solar radiation. Prolonged exposure can lead to serious health issues, including increased cancer risk. Developing effective shielding, such as using regolith from lunar or Martian surfaces or advanced materials that can absorb radiation, is crucial. These protective measures will be vital for long-term missions and settlements on other celestial bodies.

Microgravity affects not only human physiology but also the various systems necessary for life. In a microgravity environment, bone density decreases, muscle atrophy occurs, and fluid distribution in the body changes, leading to potential health complications. Research into countermeasures such as resistance exercise, nutritional interventions, and pharmacological solutions is ongoing. By 2099, space habitats may incorporate biomechanical systems that simulate gravity or utilize rotating structures to create artificial gravity, helping to mitigate these effects on inhabitants.

Sustainability is a core challenge in the quest for space habitats. The reliance on resupply missions from Earth is impractical for long-term colonization. Developing closed-loop systems that enable recycling of water, waste, and nutrients is essential. Advanced technologies for water purification, waste processing, and food production, including hydroponics and aeroponics, will play a crucial role. As humanity strives to create self-sustaining communities in space, innovative energy solutions, particularly those harnessing solar power and other renewable sources, will be integral in powering these habitats, making them viable for future generations.

Chapter 4: Innovations in Renewable Energy

Solar Power Advancements

Solar power advancements in 2099 represent a remarkable evolution in how humanity harnesses energy from the sun. Over the past several decades, innovations in photovoltaic technology have led to the development of highly efficient solar cells that can convert over 50% of sunlight into usable energy. These advancements have been propelled by breakthroughs in materials science, including the use of perovskite solar cells and tandem cell designs, which combine multiple layers of materials to capture different wavelengths of sunlight more effectively. This efficiency has enabled solar installations to provide a significant portion of the world's energy needs, contributing to a more sustainable and resilient energy infrastructure.

In urban environments, solar power has been seamlessly integrated into architecture. Buildings now feature solar skins and transparent solar windows that generate electricity without compromising aesthetics. Smart materials equipped with nanotechnology allow for dynamic adjustments to maximize energy absorption throughout the day. Additionally, solar panels have been incorporated into public infrastructure, such as roads and sidewalks, creating multifunctional surfaces that generate power while serving their primary purpose. This integration has not only enhanced energy generation but has also contributed to the reduction of urban heat islands, making cities more livable.

The role of artificial intelligence in optimizing solar power generation cannot be overstated. AI algorithms analyze real-time weather data and energy consumption patterns to predict energy output and adjust system operations accordingly. This predictive capability allows solar power plants to operate at peak efficiency, minimizing waste and maximizing energy distribution. Furthermore, AI-driven energy management systems in homes and businesses enable consumers to optimize their energy usage, shifting consumption to times when solar generation is at its highest. This synergy between AI and solar technology has ushered in a new era of smart energy management, greatly enhancing the stability of renewable energy sources.

In the context of space exploration and colonization, solar power remains a crucial component for sustainable living beyond Earth. In 2099, solar panels are deployed on lunar and Martian surfaces, providing vital energy for habitats and research stations. These extraterrestrial solar farms are designed to withstand harsh environmental conditions, utilizing advanced materials that are lightweight yet durable. The energy generated supports life support systems, scientific experiments, and even manufacturing processes, enabling self-sufficient colonies. As humanity lays the groundwork for interplanetary living, solar power continues to be an essential element of this ambitious endeavor.

The environmental monitoring capabilities of solar technology have also significantly advanced. Solar-powered drones and satellites equipped with sensors observe and analyze environmental changes, providing critical data for climate modeling and resource management. These systems facilitate real-time monitoring of deforestation, water quality, and biodiversity, allowing for proactive responses to environmental challenges. The integration of solar power with environmental monitoring technologies reflects a holistic approach to sustainability, where energy generation and ecological stewardship go hand in hand. As humanity strives to protect the last blue planet while venturing into new frontiers, solar power advancements play a pivotal role in ensuring a sustainable future for both Earth and beyond.

Wind Energy Developments

In 2099, wind energy has emerged as one of the cornerstones of sustainable power generation on Earth. The advancements in turbine technology have dramatically increased efficiency and reduced costs, making wind energy a dominant player in the global energy mix. Modern wind turbines are not only larger and more powerful but also equipped with artificial intelligence systems that optimize performance based on real-time weather data. This intelligent integration allows for the maximization of energy capture, ensuring that even the slightest breeze is harnessed effectively.

Offshore wind farms have become a significant focus of development, taking advantage of the vast, untapped potential of ocean winds. These installations are now capable of generating several gigawatts of power, enough to supply millions of homes. Innovations such as floating turbine platforms and advanced anchoring technologies have allowed for the deployment of wind farms in deeper waters, where wind speeds are higher and more consistent. This shift has not only increased energy production but has also minimized the impact on terrestrial ecosystems, reflecting a growing commitment to environmental preservation.

The role of artificial intelligence in wind energy extends beyond just turbine operation. AI algorithms are used for predictive maintenance, analyzing data from sensors embedded in turbines to forecast potential failures before they occur. This proactive approach reduces downtime and maintenance costs while ensuring that energy production remains uninterrupted. Furthermore, AI systems contribute to grid management, balancing supply and demand by predicting energy availability in real time, thus enhancing the stability of power networks.

Wind energy developments are also closely linked to advancements in energy storage technologies. As the intermittency of wind power remains a challenge, innovative solutions such as next-generation batteries and hydrogen storage systems are being deployed alongside wind farms. These technologies allow for the capture and storage of excess energy generated during peak production times, which can then be utilized during periods of low wind. This synergy between wind generation and energy storage is crucial for achieving a reliable and resilient energy system capable of supporting the needs of a growing global population.

Looking towards the future, the potential for wind energy in space exploration and colonization is becoming increasingly relevant. As humanity prepares to establish habitats beyond Earth, the principles of wind energy generation are being adapted for use in extraterrestrial environments. Concepts for utilizing solar winds or atmospheric currents on other planets are currently being researched, aiming to create sustainable energy sources for future colonies. The developments in wind energy on Earth serve not only as a model for sustainable practices but also as a stepping stone for humanity's ambitions in the cosmos, emphasizing the importance of innovation in renewable energy for both our planet and beyond.

Innovations in Energy Storage

Innovations in energy storage are crucial for addressing the challenges of the year 2099, particularly as humanity seeks to transition to sustainable energy sources while preparing for space exploration and colonization. As the demand for energy continues to escalate, driven by both a growing global population and the intensified use of advanced technologies, efficient storage solutions have emerged as a focal point of research and development. These innovations not only enhance the reliability of renewable energy systems but also facilitate their integration into everyday life, ensuring a steadier supply of power for both terrestrial and extraterrestrial applications.

One significant advancement in energy storage is the evolution of lithium-sulfur and solid-state batteries. These next-generation batteries offer higher energy densities compared to traditional lithium-ion batteries, allowing for longer-lasting energy storage capabilities. The development of solid-state technology minimizes risks associated with flammability and degradation, which have historically plagued liquid-electrolyte batteries. As a result, these innovations are set to revolutionize not only electric vehicles and portable electronics on Earth but also power sources for habitats on Mars and beyond.

In addition to advancements in battery technology, researchers have made strides in utilizing alternative materials for energy storage. Flow batteries, employing liquid electrolytes that can be scaled up for grid storage, provide a promising solution for managing intermittent renewable energy sources like solar and wind. By decoupling energy generation from storage, flow batteries enable a more flexible approach to energy management, essential for both planetary and space-based energy systems. This adaptability could support the energy needs of colonies on other planets, which will rely heavily on consistent and reliable power sources.

Moreover, artificial intelligence plays a pivotal role in optimizing energy storage systems. AI algorithms can predict energy demand and supply fluctuations, enabling smarter energy distribution and storage strategies. By analyzing vast datasets from environmental monitoring systems, AI can facilitate real-time adjustments to energy storage solutions, ensuring that energy is stored and deployed efficiently. This technology not only enhances energy management on Earth but also lays the groundwork for intelligent energy systems required in space habitats, where resource constraints demand optimal usage.

Finally, integrating energy storage innovations with smart grid technologies is essential for a sustainable future. In 2099, interconnected systems that manage energy flow, storage, and consumption will be vital for both terrestrial cities and off-world colonies. These smart grids will leverage advanced energy storage solutions to balance supply and demand effectively, ensuring resilience against power outages and enhancing the overall reliability of energy systems. By fostering a seamless connection between energy generation, storage, and consumption, humanity can build a sustainable foundation for life on Earth and the intricate habitats of space.

Chapter 5: Artificial Intelligence in Environmental Monitoring
AI Technologies for Earth Observation

AI technologies for Earth observation have become pivotal in understanding and managing our planet's changing environment. By 2099, advancements in artificial intelligence have enabled the collection and analysis of vast amounts of data from satellites, drones, and ground-based sensors. These technologies provide real-time insights into climate patterns, biodiversity, and natural resource management. The integration of AI with remote sensing has transformed traditional methods of monitoring into dynamic systems that can predict environmental changes and help mitigate their impacts.

Machine learning algorithms play a significant role in processing the intricate data derived from Earth observation systems. These algorithms analyze patterns and anomalies in climate data, enabling researchers to identify trends that may not be apparent through conventional analysis. For example, AI can track the melting of polar ice caps or shifts in vegetation cover more accurately and swiftly than human analysts. Such capabilities are crucial for developing responsive strategies that address climate-related challenges, ensuring that policymakers have access to timely information for decision-making.

Moreover, AI-driven models are essential for enhancing the accuracy of climate simulations. By utilizing historical data and current trends, these models can project future scenarios with remarkable precision. This foresight helps in planning for agricultural needs, water resource management, and urban development, ensuring that societies can adapt to the inevitable changes brought on by climate change. The ability to foresee potential crises allows governments and organizations to implement preventative measures, reducing the risk of catastrophic events.

The role of AI in environmental monitoring extends to biodiversity conservation as well. By employing computer vision and remote sensing technologies, AI can identify and track wildlife populations, monitor deforestation rates, and detect illegal poaching activities. These innovations have empowered conservationists with tools that significantly increase the efficiency of their efforts. In turn, preserving biodiversity contributes to the overall resilience of ecosystems, vital for sustaining life on Earth as well as supporting future space colonization endeavors.

As we move towards a future where space exploration and habitation become realities, the lessons learned from AI technologies for Earth observation will be invaluable. The data-driven insights gained today will inform our understanding of extraterrestrial environments and the challenges of sustaining human life beyond Earth. Harnessing AI not only helps us protect our planet but also equips us with the knowledge necessary to explore and potentially inhabit other worlds, making it an essential component of humanity's journey into the cosmos.

Predictive Analytics for Climate Change

Predictive analytics plays a crucial role in understanding and addressing the impacts of climate change, particularly as we approach the pivotal year of 2099. By leveraging vast amounts of data collected from various sources, including satellite imagery, climate models, and historical weather patterns, scientists can forecast future climate scenarios with greater accuracy. These predictions are essential for developing strategies to mitigate the effects of climate change and adapt our societies to the new realities we face. As we look to the future, predictive analytics will be instrumental in informing policy decisions and technological innovations that aim to sustain life on Earth and potentially beyond.

One of the primary applications of predictive analytics in climate science is the modeling of greenhouse gas emissions and their effects on global temperatures. By analyzing emission trends and their correlation with temperature changes, researchers can estimate future climate conditions under different scenarios of human activity. This information is vital for governments and organizations as they formulate policies to reduce emissions and promote sustainable practices. Moreover, it assists in identifying critical thresholds beyond which the effects of climate change may become catastrophic, urging immediate action to prevent irreversible damage to ecosystems.

Predictive analytics also enhances our understanding of extreme weather events, which are becoming increasingly common due to climate change. By integrating data from climate simulations and historical records, analysts can predict the likelihood and intensity of storms, droughts, and heatwaves. This capability is particularly important for disaster preparedness and response planning, allowing communities to allocate resources effectively and implement measures to protect vulnerable populations. In 2099, as we face rising sea levels and shifting weather patterns, the ability to anticipate these events will be crucial for maintaining public safety and minimizing economic disruption.

Furthermore, the intersection of artificial intelligence and predictive analytics is paving the way for innovative solutions to environmental monitoring. AI algorithms can process and analyze vast datasets far more efficiently than traditional methods, identifying trends and anomalies that may indicate impending environmental crises. This technology can facilitate real-time monitoring of ecosystems, enabling quicker responses to emerging threats such as pollution or habitat destruction. As humanity prepares for potential colonization of other planets, the lessons learned from applying predictive analytics on Earth will be invaluable in ensuring sustainable practices in new habitats.

Lastly, the insights gained from predictive analytics extend beyond immediate climate concerns, influencing broader discussions about renewable energy and space exploration. By understanding how climate change affects energy systems and resource availability, we can design renewable energy solutions that are resilient and adaptive to future conditions. Additionally, as we consider the feasibility of space habitats, predictive analytics will guide the development of sustainable living systems that mimic Earth's ecosystems. In this way, the advancements in predictive analytics not only help safeguard our planet but also serve as a blueprint for future human endeavors beyond Earth.

Case Studies of AI Applications

In the year 2099, the integration of artificial intelligence (AI) into various sectors has transformed the way humanity interacts with the environment and explores the cosmos. One prominent case study is the use of AI in environmental monitoring systems. These systems leverage advanced machine learning algorithms to analyze vast amounts of data collected from satellites and ground sensors. This data aids in tracking climate change, predicting natural disasters, and managing resources more efficiently. AI models can identify patterns in weather data, allowing for more accurate forecasts and timely responses to extreme weather events. As a result, communities are better prepared to face the challenges posed by a changing climate, enhancing resilience and sustainability on Earth.

Another significant application of AI in 2099 can be observed in the field of renewable energy. AI-driven energy management systems optimize the generation and consumption of energy from renewable sources such as solar and wind. By predicting energy demands based on consumption patterns and weather forecasts, these systems can adjust energy distribution in real-time, reducing waste and ensuring a stable supply. A specific example is the deployment of AI in smart grids, which autonomously balance energy loads and integrate diverse energy sources. This innovation not only increases the efficiency of energy use but also supports the transition to a carbon-neutral future, crucial for Earth's well-being and its quest for sustainability.

In the context of space exploration and colonization, AI has played a pivotal role in the development of autonomous spacecraft. One notable case study involves the use of AI for navigation and obstacle avoidance in interplanetary missions. These AI systems process data from onboard sensors and make real-time decisions, allowing spacecraft to navigate complex environments without human intervention. This capability is essential for missions to distant planets, where communication delays with Earth can hinder human-guided operations. The use of AI not only enhances mission safety but also enables the exploration of previously unreachable areas, expanding our understanding of the solar system and paving the way for future colonization efforts.

AI applications also extend to agriculture, particularly in the context of food production on Earth and potential off-world habitats. Advanced AI systems analyze soil health, crop conditions, and weather patterns to provide farmers with actionable insights. These technologies enable precision agriculture, which optimizes inputs such as water and fertilizers, leading to higher yields while minimizing environmental impact. In the quest for sustainable food sources in space colonization, similar AI-driven agricultural systems are being developed to support food production in controlled environments. By harnessing AI, humanity can ensure food security both on Earth and in future extraterrestrial colonies.

Finally, the ethical implications and challenges of AI applications in 2099 cannot be overlooked. As AI technologies become more embedded in environmental management, energy systems, and space exploration, questions about data privacy, decision-making transparency, and the potential for bias arise. Addressing these concerns is crucial for ensuring that AI serves as a tool for collective benefit rather than exacerbating existing inequalities. Ongoing discussions among stakeholders, including scientists, policymakers, and the public, are essential to navigate the complexities of AI integration, ensuring that technological advancements contribute positively to the future of humanity on Earth and beyond.

Chapter 6: The Role of Policy and Governance

International Space Treaties

The landscape of international space law has evolved significantly since the late 20th century, reflecting the growing interest in space exploration and the need for collaborative governance as humanity looks beyond Earth. By 2099, various international treaties have been established to regulate activities in outer space, ensuring that exploration and potential colonization are conducted in a manner that promotes peace and sustainability. The Outer Space Treaty, signed in 1967, remains the cornerstone of international space law, asserting that space is the province of all humankind and should be used for peaceful purposes. This foundational treaty has paved the way for subsequent agreements that address the complexities of a more crowded and commercially-driven space environment.

In the context of space habitats, the Moon Agreement and the Rescue Agreement are particularly relevant. The Moon Agreement, which came into force in 1984, encourages the exploration and use of the Moon and other celestial bodies for the benefit of all people, emphasizing the need for international cooperation in resource management. As humanity considers mining asteroids and colonizing the Moon or Mars, the principles enshrined in these treaties become increasingly significant. They call for a collaborative approach to resource utilization, ensuring that no single entity can claim ownership over extraterrestrial resources, thus preventing conflicts over territory and resources in a future where multiple nations and private companies may establish a presence in space.

The role of Artificial Intelligence (AI) in monitoring compliance with international treaties has become crucial in 2099. AI technologies enhance the ability to track space activities, ensuring adherence to treaties and preventing unauthorized exploitation of space resources. Advanced satellite systems equipped with AI can monitor space traffic, detect illegal activities, and provide real-time data to regulatory bodies. This not only helps in maintaining peace in space but also supports sustainable practices by ensuring that exploration efforts align with environmental standards and ethical guidelines established by international agreements.

Renewable energy technologies are also intertwined with international space treaties. As future space habitats rely on sustainable energy sources, agreements must be in place to govern the use of solar energy harnessed in space. The potential for solar power generation in orbit presents an opportunity to provide renewable energy to Earth, but it necessitates international collaboration to establish frameworks for sharing this energy equitably. Treaties that address these energy technologies will be crucial in promoting innovation while ensuring that benefits are distributed fairly among nations, particularly as the demand for clean energy escalates in the face of climate change challenges on Earth.

As humanity ventures further into space, the importance of international treaties will only grow. The establishment of clear legal frameworks fosters cooperation among nations and private entities, facilitating a shared vision for the future of space exploration and habitation. In 2099, the ongoing dialogue surrounding international space law emphasizes the need for adaptive governance that can respond to technological advancements and the dynamic nature of space activities. By ensuring that treaties evolve to address emerging challenges, the global community can work towards a future where space exploration is not only a testament to human ingenuity but also a collective endeavor that respects the rights of all and preserves the integrity of the cosmos for generations to come.

Environmental Regulations

In the year 2099, the landscape of environmental regulations has evolved dramatically in response to the pressing challenges posed by climate change, resource depletion, and biodiversity loss. Governments worldwide have implemented stringent policies aimed at safeguarding the environment while promoting sustainable development. These regulations encompass a wide array of practices, including emissions standards for industries, conservation efforts for endangered species, and guidelines for land use that prioritize ecological balance. The integration of advanced technologies into regulatory frameworks has enabled more effective monitoring and enforcement, ensuring that environmental standards are met and maintained.

Artificial intelligence plays a pivotal role in environmental monitoring and regulation enforcement. Sophisticated AI systems analyze vast amounts of data collected from satellites, sensors, and drones, providing real-time insights into environmental conditions. This technological innovation allows regulatory bodies to identify pollution sources, track deforestation rates, and monitor ecosystem health with unprecedented precision. By leveraging AI, governments can implement adaptive management strategies that respond to environmental changes more swiftly, enhancing the efficacy of regulatory measures and ensuring compliance with established standards.

Renewable energy technologies have also influenced environmental regulations substantially. As the world shifts away from fossil fuels, governments have established frameworks to encourage the adoption of clean energy sources such as solar, wind, and geothermal power. These frameworks include incentives for businesses and households to transition to renewable energy, as well as penalties for excessive carbon emissions. The success of these regulations has been bolstered by public awareness campaigns highlighting the importance of sustainability, leading to a cultural shift toward prioritizing environmental stewardship in both individual and corporate decision-making.

In the realm of space exploration and colonization, environmental regulations have taken on new dimensions. As humanity looks to expand beyond Earth, there is a growing recognition of the need to protect extraterrestrial environments. Regulatory bodies are developing guidelines to govern activities on the Moon, Mars, and beyond, ensuring that space exploration does not replicate the ecological mistakes made on Earth. These regulations focus on preventing contamination of celestial bodies, preserving potential extraterrestrial ecosystems, and managing resources sustainably, reflecting a commitment to responsible exploration that prioritizes the integrity of both terrestrial and extraterrestrial environments.

The interplay between environmental regulations and technological advancements in 2099 underscores a holistic approach to sustainability. As society grapples with the legacies of past environmental neglect, these regulations serve as a framework for fostering innovation and protecting the planet for future generations. The convergence of AI, renewable energy, and responsible space exploration creates a synergistic effect, driving progress while ensuring that the ecological balance is maintained. In this new era, the quest for space habitats is not merely about survival but also about embracing a sustainable philosophy that honors the interconnectedness of all life on Earth and beyond.

Public Participation in Policy Making

Public participation in policy making has emerged as a crucial element in the governance of environmental issues, particularly in the context of Earth in 2099. As humanity faces unprecedented challenges stemming from climate change, resource scarcity, and population pressures, the inclusion of diverse voices in the decision-making processes is essential for developing sustainable policies. In this futuristic landscape, citizens are not merely passive recipients of governmental decisions; they are active participants who influence the direction of policies that affect their lives and the health of the planet.

In 2099, technological innovations have transformed the ways in which public participation is facilitated. Digital platforms powered by advanced artificial intelligence allow for real-time engagement and feedback from citizens. Virtual town halls, interactive policy simulations, and crowd-sourced data collection have become standard practices, enabling policymakers to gauge public sentiment and incorporate community input into their strategies. This democratization of information empowers individuals to contribute their insights on environmental monitoring, renewable energy solutions, and the ethical considerations of space exploration.

The role of public participation extends beyond mere consultation; it also encompasses collaborative policymaking. In this era, governments and organizations are increasingly recognizing the value of co-creating policies with citizens. Initiatives such as participatory budgeting and community-led environmental assessments encourage people to take ownership of local challenges, fostering a sense of responsibility and stewardship. This collaborative approach not only enhances the legitimacy of policies but also ensures that they are more reflective of the community's needs and aspirations, particularly in the context of sustainable development and space colonization.

Moreover, public participation acts as a catalyst for innovation. As diverse stakeholders contribute their perspectives, new ideas and solutions emerge, particularly in areas such as renewable energy and sustainable technologies. Citizens often bring unique insights that can lead to breakthroughs in environmental practices and energy efficiency. By tapping into the collective intelligence of the community, policymakers can identify and implement strategies that are both effective and widely supported, ultimately paving the way for a more resilient planet and successful space habitats.

In conclusion, fostering public participation in policy making is essential for navigating the complexities of the challenges faced in 2099. As humanity strives to protect the Earth while exploring the cosmos, the active engagement of citizens will be vital in shaping policies that are equitable, innovative, and sustainable. By embracing new technologies and collaborative frameworks, we can ensure that the voices of the public resonate in the corridors of power, guiding us toward a brighter future both on our blue planet and beyond.

Chapter 7: Ethical Considerations in Space Colonisation
Moral Implications of Terraforming

The moral implications of terraforming extend beyond the technical challenges and environmental considerations. As humanity stands on the brink of transforming inhospitable celestial bodies into habitable environments, ethical dilemmas arise concerning our responsibilities toward these new worlds. The prospect of altering the atmosphere, geology, and ecosystems of planets like Mars or moons such as Europa prompts questions about the sanctity of untouched ecosystems. Should humanity impose its will on these celestial bodies, or do they have an inherent value that deserves protection, similar to the preservation efforts we undertake on Earth?

One significant moral consideration is the potential for unintended consequences. In our quest to create habitable conditions, we risk disrupting any existing life forms or ecosystems that might already exist, even in microscopic forms. The risk of contamination and the ethical duty to avoid harming alien biospheres present a complex challenge. The precautionary principle, which advocates for caution in the face of uncertainty, must be a guiding philosophy in our terraforming endeavors. This principle urges us to consider the possible repercussions of our actions and questions whether we have the right to experiment with environments that may harbor unknown forms of life.

Moreover, the concept of terraforming raises issues of equity and justice. As wealthy nations and corporations lead the charge in space exploration, the benefits of terraforming may not be equitably distributed. The creation of new habitats could exacerbate existing inequalities on Earth, where resources are already scarce for many. The moral implications of prioritizing the colonization of other worlds over addressing pressing issues such as poverty, climate change, and resource management on our home planet cannot be overlooked. It is crucial to engage in discussions that ensure the voices of marginalized communities are heard in these decisions, promoting inclusivity in the governance of space exploration.

Additionally, the potential for terraforming to serve as a "backup plan" for humanity raises ethical concerns about our stewardship of

Earth. Relying on the idea that we can simply migrate to another planet if we fail to protect our own environment may diminish our sense of responsibility for Earth. This mindset risks perpetuating harmful practices that lead to environmental degradation. The moral obligation to care for our planet must be prioritized, as the lessons learned from Earth's ecological crises should inform our approach to terraforming. In this context, terraforming should not be seen as an escape route but rather as a complementary effort to safeguard and restore our original home.

Ultimately, the moral implications of terraforming call for a collective reevaluation of our values and priorities as we venture into the cosmos. As we develop technologies for space exploration and colonization, we must ensure that ethical considerations are woven into the fabric of our missions. Engaging in dialogue about the responsibilities we bear toward other worlds and the consequences of our actions will be essential in shaping a future that honors both our aspirations and our ethical obligations. In doing so, we can navigate the complexities of terraforming with a sense of purpose and integrity, fostering a harmonious relationship between humanity and the universe.

Rights of Potential Extraterrestrial Life

The emergence of potential extraterrestrial life forms raises profound questions about their rights and the ethical implications of human interaction with these entities. As we venture beyond Earth in 2099, our understanding of life itself is challenged by the discovery of microorganisms and complex organisms on other celestial bodies. This leads to discussions on whether these life forms should be granted rights similar to those we uphold for sentient beings on Earth. The framework for these rights must consider not only the biological characteristics of extraterrestrial life but also our moral responsibilities as stewards of the universe.

Legal frameworks on Earth have long been rooted in human-centric values, but the advent of extraterrestrial discovery necessitates a shift toward a more inclusive perspective. In 2099, discussions at international forums and space agencies have begun to address the rights of potential extraterrestrial life, focusing on the need for a universal declaration that recognizes their existence and intrinsic value. This is not merely a philosophical endeavor; it has practical implications for how humanity approaches space exploration and colonization. Establishing rights for extraterrestrial life could prevent exploitation and promote a more ethical approach to planetary protection.

Technological innovations play a crucial role in our understanding of potential extraterrestrial ecosystems. Advanced artificial intelligence systems are employed in monitoring environments on Mars, Europa, and other celestial bodies. These technologies help scientists distinguish between abiotic and biotic processes, facilitating the identification of life forms. As we develop these tools, it becomes imperative to incorporate ethical considerations into their design and implementation. AI systems must not only gather data but also be programmed to respect the rights of discovered life forms, ensuring that humanity approaches these new worlds with caution and respect.

Moreover, the concept of rights for extraterrestrial life intersects with environmental monitoring initiatives on Earth itself. The lessons we learn about protecting extraterrestrial ecosystems can inform our actions on our home planet. By establishing a precedent for respecting life beyond Earth, we can cultivate a deeper appreciation for biodiversity and conservation efforts here. As we face environmental challenges, the principles guiding our interaction with potential extraterrestrial life can inspire a more holistic approach to environmental stewardship, emphasizing interconnectedness among all forms of life.

In conclusion, the rights of potential extraterrestrial life challenge humanity to reconsider its ethical frameworks and responsibilities as we explore the cosmos. As we stand on the brink of a new era in 2099, the establishment of rights for extraterrestrial entities could herald a transformative shift in our approach to space exploration, technological development, and environmental ethics. By embracing a forward-thinking perspective that prioritizes respect for all forms of life, we can foster a more sustainable and ethically sound exploration of the universe, ensuring that our legacy as a species is one of stewardship rather than exploitation.

Responsibilities to Future Generations

In the context of Earth in 2099, the responsibilities we hold towards future generations are paramount. As we grapple with the consequences of climate change, resource depletion, and biodiversity loss, it becomes increasingly clear that our actions today will shape the planet for those who come after us. The stewardship of Earth involves not only preserving the environment but also ensuring that the technological advancements we pursue are sustainable and equitable. The decisions made now regarding renewable energy technologies, environmental monitoring through artificial intelligence, and the exploration of space habitats will reverberate for generations to come.

The transition to renewable energy sources is a critical aspect of our responsibility to future generations. In 2099, the world has made significant strides in harnessing solar, wind, and other sustainable energy sources. However, the legacy of fossil fuel dependence still looms large, and the impacts of past energy choices can still be felt. To ensure a livable planet for the future, we must prioritize investments in innovations that not only reduce carbon emissions but also promote energy equity. By fostering technologies that are accessible and affordable, we can empower communities to thrive without compromising the planet's health.

Artificial intelligence plays a transformative role in environmental monitoring, offering us the tools necessary to understand and mitigate the impacts of climate change. In 2099, AI systems are utilized to track ecosystem changes, predict natural disasters, and optimize resource management. However, this technology must be developed and deployed with a sense of ethical responsibility. Ensuring data privacy and preventing biases in AI algorithms are crucial to maintaining public trust. By prioritizing transparency and accountability in AI applications, we can create a future where technology serves humanity and the planet, rather than exacerbating existing inequalities.

As we consider the prospect of space exploration and colonization, our responsibilities expand beyond Earth. The search for habitable environments on other planets raises ethical questions about our role as stewards of the cosmos. In 2099, discussions surrounding planetary protection and the prevention of contamination have become central to space missions. We must approach the exploration of space with the same caution and respect we owe to Earth. This involves developing stringent protocols to ensure that we do not repeat the mistakes of environmental degradation that have plagued our home planet. Our ventures into space must be guided by principles that honor both our present and future responsibilities.

Ultimately, the concept of intergenerational equity emphasizes that our choices today must reflect consideration for the wellbeing of future inhabitants of Earth and beyond. As we navigate the complex challenges of our time, we must cultivate a mindset that prioritizes long-term sustainability over short-term gains. By embracing innovative technologies, fostering ethical practices in AI and environmental stewardship, and approaching space exploration with caution, we can lay the groundwork for a thriving planet. The choices we make now are not merely about survival; they are about ensuring that future generations inherit a world where they can flourish, both on Earth and in the broader universe.

Chapter 8: The Future of Humanity on Earth and Beyond
Coexistence with Nature

In the year 2099, humanity's relationship with nature has evolved significantly, driven by the urgent need to coexist with the planet rather than exploit it. As the effects of climate change became increasingly catastrophic in the late 21st century, society recognized that sustainable living was not merely an option but a necessity for survival. This shift in mindset has led to innovative approaches that integrate technology with ecological principles, allowing urban environments to harmonize with natural ecosystems. The design of cities as biophilic habitats, where greenery and wildlife thrive alongside human activity, illustrates this new paradigm of coexistence.

Technological innovations have played a crucial role in fostering this harmony. Renewable energy sources, such as advanced solar panels and wind turbines, have become ubiquitous, providing clean energy without compromising the environment. The development of energy-efficient infrastructures, including vertical gardens and green roofs, has minimized urban heat effects and improved air quality. Furthermore, smart grids powered by artificial intelligence enable real-time energy management, optimizing consumption while reducing waste. These technologies not only help to mitigate climate change but also create spaces where nature and humanity can thrive together.

Artificial intelligence has further enhanced our ability to coexist with nature through environmental monitoring and management systems. AI-driven sensors are deployed across various ecosystems to collect data on biodiversity, soil health, and water quality. This information allows for proactive measures to protect endangered species and restore degraded habitats. Additionally, AI algorithms can predict environmental changes, enabling better preparedness for natural disasters and ensuring sustainable resource management. By leveraging technology in this manner, humanity can make informed decisions that prioritize ecological balance while fulfilling societal needs.

The integration of nature into everyday life is also evident in agricultural practices. Vertical farming and permaculture have gained traction as sustainable alternatives to traditional farming methods. These practices not only maximize land use but also reduce transportation emissions, as food can be grown closer to urban centers. The use of drones for pollination and crop monitoring exemplifies how technology can enhance agricultural productivity while minimizing ecological footprints. This collaboration between technological innovation and nature underscores a profound shift towards a more sustainable food system that respects the earth's limits.

As humanity looks towards colonizing other planets, the lessons learned from coexisting with nature on Earth will be invaluable. The principles of sustainability, resilience, and respect for natural systems will guide future endeavors in space exploration. Creating self-sustaining habitats on other planets will require an understanding of closed-loop systems and ecological balance, mirroring the practices developed on Earth. By embracing coexistence with nature as a foundational principle, we can ensure that our quest for space does not repeat the mistakes of our past but instead paves the way for a harmonious existence with both our home planet and any new worlds we may inhabit.

The Vision for Interstellar Travel

The vision for interstellar travel in the year 2099 is a bold and ambitious pursuit, spurred by humanity's urgent need to find alternatives to a dwindling Earth. As climate change and resource depletion have reached critical levels, the exploration of distant star systems has become not only a dream but a necessity. Researchers and scientists are now actively working on advanced propulsion systems that could one day take us beyond our solar system. Concepts like warp drives, which theoretically allow for faster-than-light travel, and generation ships, capable of housing entire communities for extended periods, are being explored with renewed vigor.

Technological innovations in renewable energy are pivotal to realizing this vision. As fossil fuels become increasingly obsolete, solar sails, fusion reactors, and other sustainable energy sources are being developed to power spacecraft on long voyages. Solar sails, utilizing the pressure of sunlight, could propel ships to distant stars, while fusion energy promises a nearly limitless supply of power for both propulsion and life support systems. These advancements not only support interstellar missions but also have the potential to transform energy generation and consumption on Earth, contributing to a more sustainable future.

Artificial intelligence plays a crucial role in the planning and execution of interstellar missions. AI systems are being designed to handle the complexities of space travel, from navigation through unknown territories to managing onboard ecosystems for human crews. The integration of AI in spacecraft can enhance decision-making processes, optimize resource usage, and ensure the safety of crew members on long-duration missions. Furthermore, AI-driven environmental monitoring systems are essential for assessing the viability of potential exoplanets for colonization, analyzing atmospheric conditions, and identifying potential hazards.

The prospect of establishing habitats on other planets raises significant ethical and environmental considerations. As humanity reaches for the stars, it is vital to ensure that we do not repeat the mistakes of our past, particularly in terms of exploiting new worlds without regard for their ecosystems. This calls for a careful examination of our responsibilities as stewards of both Earth and any new territories we may inhabit. Policies and frameworks need to be developed to govern interstellar exploration, ensuring that we approach this frontier with the same respect and caution that we should have for our own planet.

As we look towards the future, the vision of interstellar travel represents not just a technological challenge but a profound shift in our understanding of humanity's place in the universe. The quest for new homes beyond Earth is intertwined with our efforts to address pressing issues at home. By investing in sustainable technologies, harnessing the power of AI, and cultivating an ethos of environmental stewardship, we can pave the way for a new era of exploration that not only saves humanity but also enriches our collective experience as we venture into the cosmos.

Preparing for the Unknown

Preparing for the unknown in the context of Earth in 2099 is an essential aspect of humanity's journey toward space habitats and sustainable living. As climate change and resource depletion become more pressing challenges, the need to explore beyond our planet intensifies. The development of space habitats is not merely about finding new places to live; it is about ensuring the survival of humanity and creating a blueprint for sustainable living both on Earth and beyond. This subchapter examines the various dimensions of preparing for the unknown, focusing on technological innovations, environmental monitoring, and the role of artificial intelligence.

Technological innovations for renewable energy will play a pivotal role in preparing for the unknown. In 2099, the reliance on fossil fuels has diminished significantly, giving way to advanced energy systems that harness solar, wind, and other renewable sources. The ability to generate clean energy efficiently is crucial for sustaining life in space habitats. Breakthroughs in energy storage technologies, such as high-capacity batteries and supercapacitors, allow for the efficient use of energy generated from renewable sources. These technologies not only support human habitation in space but also provide a sustainable energy grid for Earth, ensuring that communities can thrive amid the uncertainties of climate change.

Artificial intelligence (AI) will be an indispensable tool in navigating the unknown challenges of space colonization and environmental monitoring. In 2099, AI systems are integrated into nearly every aspect of daily life, driving advancements in predictive analytics and decision-making processes. These systems can monitor environmental conditions, identify potential hazards, and develop strategies for managing resources effectively. For space habitats, AI plays a critical role in optimizing life support systems, ensuring that air, water, and food supplies are maintained efficiently. By harnessing the power of AI, humanity can better prepare for unforeseen challenges, whether on Earth or in the depths of space. Environmental monitoring technologies have advanced significantly, enabling real-time data collection and analysis. In 2099, sophisticated satellite systems and drones equipped with sensors provide comprehensive insights into Earth's ecosystems and climate patterns. This data is vital for understanding the impacts of human activity and natural phenomena on our environment. By continuously monitoring changes in atmospheric conditions, biodiversity, and resource availability, scientists can develop adaptive strategies to mitigate environmental degradation. Furthermore, this information is essential for planning and constructing space habitats, as it informs the selection of locations that are resilient to environmental fluctuations.

Preparing for the unknown also involves fostering a mindset of adaptability and innovation. In a rapidly changing world, the ability to pivot and respond to new challenges is crucial. Education and public awareness campaigns play a vital role in equipping individuals with the knowledge and skills necessary to thrive in uncertain times. Encouraging collaboration between governments, private sectors, and research institutions can lead to innovative solutions that address both terrestrial and extraterrestrial challenges. By cultivating a culture of resilience and foresight, humanity can ensure that it is prepared for the unknown, embracing the opportunities that lie ahead while safeguarding the future of our planet and beyond.

After having sneaked the narrative into the future and what might have happened, now let us step backwards and see what we can do between now (year 2025) to 2099. The importance of this assumptions (in my opinion) is that there are many things that can be done to correct the course of the wrong trajectory that the earth is almost trending on environmentary.

Chapter 9: Terraforming tomorrow: a guide to creating habitable worlds by 2099

The Concept of Terraforming

The concept of terraforming refers to the deliberate modification of a planet's environment to make it habitable for Earth-like life forms. This process encompasses a variety of techniques aimed at altering the atmosphere, temperature, surface topography, and ecology of a celestial body to create conditions conducive to human life. By the year 2099, advancements in technology and a deeper understanding of planetary systems will allow us to implement terraforming strategies on a scale previously deemed impossible. The focus will be on transforming inhospitable environments, such as Mars or the moons of Jupiter and Saturn, into vibrant ecosystems capable of supporting human and terrestrial life.

Soil enhancement methods will play a pivotal role in extraterrestrial agriculture. These techniques will involve the introduction of nutrients and organic matter to create fertile soils suitable for growing crops in alien environments. Strategies may include the use of microbial inoculants, biochar, and hydroponics, which can optimise plant growth while minimising resource use. By employing these methods, terraforming efforts will not only ensure food security for off-world colonies but also contribute to the overall stability of the local ecosystem. The ability to cultivate crops will be essential for long-term habitation and will require innovative approaches to soil management in varied extraterrestrial conditions.

Water sourcing and management will be another critical aspect of terraforming. Access to water is fundamental to sustaining life, and innovative methods will be developed to harvest and manage this vital resource in space habitats. Techniques such as extracting water from the ice caps of Mars or using advanced filtration systems to recycle wastewater will be essential. Additionally, the establishment of closed-loop water systems will ensure that water is efficiently utilised and reused, reducing the need for external supplies. Effective water management will not only support agriculture but also maintain human health and sanitation in off-world colonies.

Energy generation systems will be integral to supporting sustainable living in extraterrestrial environments. By 2099, technologies such as solar panels, nuclear reactors, and potentially even fusion power will be harnessed to provide reliable energy sources. These systems will need to be resilient and adaptable to the harsh conditions of space, ensuring that energy is consistently available for both daily needs and terraforming efforts. The development of efficient energy solutions will facilitate the operation of life support systems, agricultural endeavors, and construction projects, creating a self-sustaining infrastructure for human habitation.

Lastly, the ethical considerations surrounding terraforming will shape policies and frameworks that guide these endeavors. The potential for unintended consequences on alien ecosystems and the moral implications of altering another world will demand careful consideration. Policymakers will need to establish guidelines that protect both the integrity of extraterrestrial environments and the rights of future inhabitants. By fostering a collaborative approach that includes scientific, ethical, and public perspectives, terraforming can be pursued responsibly, ensuring that the legacy of humanity's expansion into the cosmos is one of stewardship and respect for the universe.

Historical context and advances in technology

The concept of terraforming has its roots in science fiction, but historical developments in technology have gradually transformed these imaginative ideas into actionable plans. The notion of altering the environment of another planet to make it habitable gained traction in the mid-20th century, spurred by advancements in space exploration and planetary science. As humanity's understanding of celestial bodies expanded through missions to Mars and beyond, scientists began to consider practical methods for transforming these harsh environments. Early theorists proposed various techniques, such as introducing greenhouse gases to warm a planet's atmosphere or creating artificial magnetic fields to protect against solar radiation. These foundational ideas set the stage for the more sophisticated approaches we explore today.

The late 20th and early 21st centuries saw significant advancements in technology that paved the way for terraforming initiatives. Techniques in soil enhancement, for example, evolved rapidly with the advent of genetic engineering and bioremediation. Researchers began experimenting with microbial inoculants and biochar to improve soil quality, which is crucial for extraterrestrial agriculture. As we look to 2099, the integration of 'synthetic' biology and automated systems will likely enable the creation of nutrient-rich soils on barren worlds, allowing for the cultivation of crops adapted to alien conditions. This technological evolution not only enhances food production but also contributes to the overall sustainability of off-world colonies.

Water sourcing and management have also been revolutionised through innovative technologies. The discovery of water ice on Mars and the potential for extracting water from subsurface sources have shifted the paradigm of interplanetary resource management. Advanced techniques such as atmospheric harvesting and the use of advanced filtration systems will be essential in ensuring a reliable water supply for future habitats. By 2099, we can expect the implementation of closed-loop water systems that recycle and purify water through cutting-edge filtration and purification technologies, minimizing waste and maximizing efficiency in extraterrestrial environments.

Energy generation systems are another critical component of sustainable living on other planets. Historically, reliance on fossil fuels has been the norm on Earth, but the push for renewable energy has spurred innovations in solar, wind, and nuclear power. For off-world colonies, solar energy is particularly promising due to the abundance of sunlight in space. By 2099, advancements in energy storage and conversion will enable colonies to harness solar power effectively. Moreover, technologies such as fusion energy could provide a virtually limitless power source, ensuring that habitats can support growing populations and advanced technologies without depleting resources.

As we advance toward the goal of terraforming, ethical considerations and policy frameworks will play a pivotal role in guiding these endeavours. The historical context of terraforming discussions has often been marred by concerns over environmental impact and the potential consequences of altering extraterrestrial ecosystems. By 2099, it will be crucial to establish comprehensive guidelines that address these issues, incorporating principles of responsibility and sustainability in terraforming practices. This approach will not only ensure the protection of potential alien life forms but also foster a collaborative spirit among nations and organisations involved in the quest for new habitable worlds. As we navigate the complexities of terraforming, a balanced understanding of technology, ethics, and policy will be essential in shaping a future that harmonises human ambition with the preservation of the cosmos.

Chapter 10: Terrestrial Terraforming for space habitation

Principles of Terraforming

Principles of terraforming revolve around the concept of transforming an inhospitable environment into a habitable one, particularly on other planets or moons. This process is grounded in a deep understanding of planetary science, biology, and engineering. The primary goal is to create conditions that support human life, which includes establishing breathable atmospheres, suitable climates, and viable ecosystems. Achieving these goals requires integrating various scientific disciplines, including atmospheric chemistry, ecology, and environmental engineering, to ensure that every aspect of the transformation is sustainable and effective in the long term.

Soil enhancement methods play a critical role in extraterrestrial agriculture, as nutrient-rich soil is essential for plant growth and food production. Techniques such as in-situ resource utilisation, where native materials are converted into usable soil, will be pivotal. This may involve the application of microbial inoculants to enrich the soil with necessary nutrients or the engineering of soil structures to improve water retention and aeration. Additionally, the incorporation of organic waste recycling systems will not only enhance soil quality but also promote a closed-loop system that minimises waste and maximises resource efficiency within off-world colonies.

Water sourcing and management is another fundamental principle of terraforming, particularly in creating sustainable habitats. Identifying and extracting water resources from ice deposits or subsurface aquifers will be essential for supporting life. Advanced techniques for water purification and recycling will ensure that water remains a renewable resource. Engineers and scientists will need to develop efficient systems for capturing atmospheric moisture or utilising hydroponics and aquaponics in agriculture to optimise water usage. A thorough understanding of local hydrology will guide these efforts, ensuring that water management systems are robust and adaptable to changing conditions.

Energy generation systems are vital for sustaining life in extraterrestrial environments, where traditional energy sources are often unavailable. Innovations in solar power, nuclear energy, and potentially even fusion technology will be crucial. The design of energy systems must focus on reliability and efficiency to support habitats, agricultural systems, and life support technologies. Moreover, energy efficiency must be a guiding principle, ensuring that every aspect of planetary habitation is designed to minimise consumption while maximising output. This approach will help create a self-sustaining community capable of thriving in its new environment.

Finally, ethical considerations and policy frameworks are indispensable in the discourse of terraforming. As humanity embarks on the journey of transforming other worlds, it must address the potential consequences of these actions on existing ecosystems and potential life forms. Policies must be established to govern the responsible use of technology and resources, ensuring that terraforming efforts do not lead to irreversible harm. A collaborative approach involving scientists, ethicists, policymakers, and the public will be essential in creating guidelines that prioritise sustainability and respect for alien environments. In doing so, humanity can aspire to create not just habitable worlds but also equitable and just societies within them.

Case studies: Mars and Venus

The exploration of Mars and Venus serves as a pivotal foundation in the discussion of terraforming and the potential creation of habitable worlds. Mars, often referred to as the "Red Planet," presents unique opportunities due to its similarities to Earth, such as the presence of polar ice caps and a day length that closely resembles our own. The potential for soil enhancement methods on Mars is particularly promising. Research has suggested that Martian regolith could be treated with organic compounds and microorganisms to improve its fertility, enabling the cultivation of genetically modified crops designed to thrive in the planet's harsh conditions. Such advancements are critical for developing sustainable agriculture that could support future Martian colonies.

Conversely, Venus offers a contrasting case study due to its extreme atmospheric conditions. The thick, toxic atmosphere composed mainly of carbon dioxide, with clouds of sulfuric acid, poses significant challenges for any potential terraforming efforts. However, concepts for floating habitats in the upper atmosphere have emerged, where temperatures and pressures are more Earth-like. These biodomes would require innovative design solutions to manage ecosystems that could function in low gravity and high-pressure environments. The study of Venus highlights not only the engineering challenges involved but also the ethical considerations surrounding the manipulation of a planet that may harbour its own forms of life, albeit in a very different context.

Water sourcing and management are crucial components of any terraforming endeavor. On Mars, potential water ice reserves in its polar regions and subsurface could be accessed through advanced drilling techniques, making it feasible to create sustainable water systems. These systems would need to integrate with energy generation technologies, such as solar panels or nuclear reactors, to ensure a consistent supply of energy for water extraction and processing. In contrast, Venus's abundant atmospheric water vapour could be harvested using advanced condensation techniques, though this would necessitate robust energy solutions to support such operations in its hostile environment.

Energy generation systems are essential for supporting life in off-world habitats. Mars benefits from solar energy, given its proximity to the Sun and the availability of solar panels that could be deployed on its surface. However, the efficiency of these systems could be affected by dust storms that frequently envelop the planet (a bit of this happens in the Middle East and towns within proximity to Sahara desert). For Venus, the challenge lies in developing energy systems that can withstand extreme temperatures while harnessing the thick atmosphere's kinetic energy. These innovative solutions will not only provide necessary power for habitats but also play a role in the overall sustainability of human life in these environments.

As humanity moves towards the potential colonization of these planets, it is imperative to consider the long-term implications of our actions. This includes understanding the ecological impact of introducing Earth organisms to alien environments and the potential for irreversible changes to these ecosystems.

Establishing ethical guidelines and policy frameworks will be essential for ensuring that terraforming efforts are conducted responsibly, balancing the pursuit of human habitation with the preservation of extraterrestrial environments.

Timeline for Terraforming initiatives by 2099

The timeline for terraforming initiatives by 2099 reflects a comprehensive approach to creating habitable environments beyond Earth. By the mid-21st century, significant advancements in space technology will have laid the groundwork for initial terraforming efforts. The first phase, spanning from 2025 to 2045, will focus on establishing human presence on Mars and the Moon. During this period, robotic missions will test soil enhancement methods, which include the introduction of Earth microorganisms to improve soil fertility and the development of hydroponic systems for extraterrestrial agriculture. Water sourcing will also be a priority, with innovations in ice mining and atmospheric water harvesting paving the way for sustainable water management systems.

Following the establishment of initial habitats, the second phase from 2045 to 2070 will see the deployment of biodomes designed for ecosystem management. These biodomes will serve as controlled environments that support diverse plant and animal life, essential for long-term space habitation. During this period, researchers will focus on the genetic modification of plants to thrive in alien environments, utilizing advanced CRISPR technology to enhance resilience against harsh conditions. Simultaneously, energy generation systems, including solar arrays and nuclear reactors, will be implemented to ensure reliable power sources for off-world colonies.

By 2070, the third phase will initiate large-scale terraforming projects, which will involve altering planetary atmospheres and climates. A key aspect of this phase will be the introduction of engineered microorganisms that can produce oxygen and sequester carbon dioxide, thus gradually transforming the atmosphere of Mars and other celestial bodies. The construction of infrastructure using advanced materials will also commence, utilising local resources to reduce dependency on Earth for construction materials. Innovations in construction methods will be essential to build sustainable habitats that can withstand the unique challenges of extraterrestrial environments.

As we approach 2099, the final phase will focus on refining terraforming strategies and solidifying terraforming ethics and policy frameworks. This period will involve international collaboration to establish ethical guidelines for terraforming initiatives, ensuring that the rights of potential extraterrestrial life forms are respected while addressing the needs of human settlers. Health and medical innovations will also play a critical role, with advancements in telemedicine and biotechnology enhancing the quality of life for off-world inhabitants. The integration of these innovations will create a holistic approach to ensuring the health and sustainability of human life in new environments.

By 2099, the cumulative efforts of these initiatives will lead to the establishment of vibrant, self-sustaining colonies on other planets. The timeline for terraforming initiatives emphasises a gradual process that prioritises scientific research, ethical considerations, and sustainable practices. As humanity embarks on this unprecedented journey, the lessons learned from each phase will inform future endeavours in space habitation, ultimately transforming our understanding of life beyond earth and ensuring a viable future for generations to come.

Chapter 11: Soil enhancement methods for extraterrestrial agriculture

Soil composition and quality

Soil composition and quality are critical factors in the success of terraforming efforts aimed at creating habitable environments on other planets. For extraterrestrial agriculture to flourish, it is essential to understand the fundamental components of soil, which include minerals, organic matter, water, air, and living organisms. Each of these elements plays a vital role in supporting plant growth and maintaining a balanced ecosystem. When selecting a location for a new colony, understanding the existing soil characteristics will inform decisions about necessary enhancements and modifications to create an environment suitable for sustaining life.

The mineral content of soil varies greatly across different celestial bodies. For instance, Martian soil is primarily composed of iron oxides, silica, and various salts, while lunar regolith is rich in silicates and lacks organic material. These differences necessitate tailored soil enhancement methods to improve fertility and structure. Techniques such as adding biochar to increase nutrient retention or employing microorganisms to promote organic matter breakdown can be pivotal in transforming inhospitable soils into fertile ground for agriculture. Additionally, the incorporation of locally sourced materials could reduce the need for transporting resources from Earth, making the terraforming process more sustainable.

Water sourcing and management are closely linked to soil quality. The availability of water impacts soil structure, nutrient availability, and the overall health of plants. In many extraterrestrial environments, water may be scarce or exist in forms that are not readily usable for agriculture. Innovative techniques such as atmospheric water harvesting or recycling wastewater can provide the necessary moisture for enhanced soil systems. Furthermore, understanding how water interacts with soil minerals and organic matter is crucial for developing irrigation systems that maximize efficiency and minimize waste in off-world colonies.

The potential impact on native ecosystems, even if they are minimal or non-existent, raises questions about our responsibilities as terraformers. Establishing policy frameworks that govern the use of genetic modification to create plants suited for alien conditions, as well as guidelines for soil enhancement methods, will be essential to ensure that terraforming efforts are conducted responsibly. Engaging with a diverse range of stakeholders, including scientists, ethicists, and the public, will foster a collaborative approach to creating habitable worlds while addressing moral implications and promoting sustainability.

Techniques for soil enrichment

Techniques for soil enrichment play a crucial role in the success of terrestrial terraforming and the establishment of sustainable agriculture on extraterrestrial worlds. As human exploration extends beyond earth, it becomes imperative to develop methods that enhance soil quality in environments where natural processes are either absent or significantly altered. These techniques focus on improving soil fertility, structure, and moisture retention to support plant growth in harsh, alien landscapes.

In addition to organic amendments, mineral supplementation is essential for addressing nutrient deficiencies often found in extraterrestrial soils. Essential elements like nitrogen, phosphorus, and potassium can be introduced through various means, including the use of chemical fertilisers or slow-release mineral compounds. Moreover, the incorporation of mycorrhizal fungi can enhance nutrient uptake for plants, allowing them to thrive even in less-than-ideal soil conditions. This symbiotic relationship between fungi and plant roots not only improves nutrient availability but also increases plant tolerance to environmental stresses.

Water management is another critical component of soil enrichment strategies. Techniques such as constructing swales, rain gardens, and other water-retaining structures can help capture and hold moisture in arid environments. The use of hydrogels or water-retaining polymers can further improve moisture retention in the soil, providing an essential resource for plant growth. Implementing efficient irrigation systems, such as drip irrigation, can also ensure that water is used judiciously, minimising waste and maximising crop yields in extraterrestrial agriculture.

Implementing hydroponics and aeroponics

Implementing hydroponics and aeroponics represents a pivotal advancement in the effort to create sustainable agricultural systems for extraterrestrial environments. As we explore the challenges of terraforming and establishing off-world colonies, these soil-less growing techniques offer adaptable solutions that maximise resource efficiency in space habitats. Hydroponics involves growing plants in nutrient-rich water solutions, while aeroponics utilises mist to deliver nutrients directly to plant roots. These methods are not only space-efficient but also reduce the need for extensive water supplies, a critical consideration given the limited availability of liquid water in many extraterrestrial settings.

Finally, the ethical implications of genetic modification and the selection of plant species for these systems must be addressed. As we engineer crops to thrive in extraterrestrial environments, it is vital to consider the potential ecological impacts, as well as the moral responsibilities associated with altering life forms. Establishing policy frameworks around these innovations will help guide the development and implementation of hydroponics and aeroponics, ensuring that they contribute positively to the holistic ecosystem management of off-world colonies. By integrating these advanced agricultural techniques, we can pave the way for sustainable living on other planets, ultimately fulfilling the vision of creating habitable worlds by 2099.

Chapter 12: Water sourcing and management in space habitats

Water recovery systems

Water Recovery Systems play a critical role in the sustainability of extraterrestrial habitats. As humanity extends its reach into the cosmos, the ability to efficiently source, manage, and recycle water becomes paramount for the survival of off-world colonies. Given the scarcity of liquid water in many environments outside Earth, innovative systems designed for water recovery will not only support human life but also enable agricultural practices essential for long-term habitation. These systems must be robust, adaptable, and capable of functioning in diverse extraterrestrial conditions.

One of the foundational technologies in water recovery is the process of condensation. This involves capturing moisture from the atmosphere, a method previously utilised in arid regions on earth. In space habitats, advanced condensation systems can be engineered to harvest water vapor from the air generated by human activity, vegetation, and even from the moisture released during food preparation. By optimising the collection efficiency of these systems, habitats can significantly reduce their reliance on external water sources, which may be limited or unavailable.

Furthermore, the integration of biological water recovery systems can enhance water management in extraterrestrial environments. These systems utilise engineered microorganisms or plants that can extract moisture from the soil or air. For instance, certain genetically modified plants could be designed to thrive in alien soils while simultaneously pulling moisture from the atmosphere and returning it to the habitat's water supply. This not only supports water recovery but also contributes to the overall ecosystem management within biodomes, promoting a symbiotic relationship between water recovery and agricultural productivity.

In addition to natural methods, mechanical systems such as reverse osmosis and advanced filtration techniques will be essential for purifying any collected water. These systems will need to be energy-efficient, as energy generation is another critical aspect of sustainable living in space. By combining water recovery with renewable energy sources, habitats can create a closed-loop system that maximizes resource efficiency. This synergy between water recovery and energy generation ensures that off-world colonies can thrive while minimising their ecological footprint.

Ultimately, the development and implementation of effective water recovery systems are integral to the success of terraforming efforts. These systems not only provide the necessary water for human survival and agricultural practices but also contribute to the broader goals of creating self-sustaining ecosystems on other planets. As we move towards the ambitious goal of establishing permanent human presence beyond earth by 2099, investing in innovative water recovery technologies will be essential for overcoming the challenges of extraterrestrial habitation and ensuring a sustainable future for humanity in the cosmos.

Desalination techniques for off-world use

Desalination techniques will play a crucial role in supporting human life and agriculture on off-world colonies, particularly in environments where traditional water sourcing methods are impractical. As terraforming efforts progress, the availability of water becomes essential for sustaining ecosystems and enabling human habitation. Various desalination methods can be adapted to extraterrestrial conditions, focusing on efficiency, energy consumption, and scalability. Understanding these methods will be vital for future settlers to ensure a reliable water supply in their new environments.

Reverse osmosis is one of the most promising desalination techniques for off-world use. This method employs a semipermeable membrane to separate salt and impurities from water, allowing only clean water to pass through. In extraterrestrial settings, where energy resources may be limited, the energy efficiency of reverse osmosis systems can be optimised by utilising solar power or other renewable energy sources available on the planet. Additionally, advancements in membrane technology may lead to more effective filtration processes that can operate under varying pressures, a necessary adaptation for different planetary atmospheres.

Another viable desalination technique is solar distillation, which harnesses solar energy to evaporate water and subsequently condense it into a separate container. This method could be particularly advantageous on planets with high solar irradiance, such as Mars. By constructing solar stills or larger-scale solar distillation plants, colonies can convert brackish or saline water sources into potable water. The simplicity and low energy requirements of this method make it an attractive option for off-world environments where complex infrastructure might be challenging to establish.

Electrodialysis represents a more advanced method that utilises electric fields to drive ions through selective ion exchange membranes, effectively separating salt from water. This technique can be particularly useful in scenarios where energy availability is less of a concern, such as in colonies equipped with robust energy generation systems. Electrodialysis could also be integrated with other processes, such as water recycling systems, to create a more comprehensive water management strategy that supports long-term sustainability in extraterrestrial habitats.

The development and implementation of these desalination techniques must also consider the unique challenges posed by off-world environments. Factors such as extreme temperatures, radiation exposure, and limited resources necessitate innovative engineering solutions that are both resilient and adaptable. As research progresses in this field, the intersection of technology, resource management, and environmental stewardship will be essential in ensuring the success of human settlement on other planets, paving the way for thriving ecosystems and sustainable living in our solar system.

Water recycling and conservation are crucial components in the quest for sustainable living on extraterrestrial environments. As humanity embarks on the journey of terraforming planets for habitation, the management of water resources will be one of the primary challenges to ensure a self-sufficient ecosystem. By 2099, innovative technologies and strategies will need to be employed to recycle and conserve water effectively, making the most of every precious drop in off-world colonies.

One of the most promising methods for water recycling involves advanced filtration systems that can purify wastewater generated by humans and agriculture. These systems will utilise cutting-edge nanotechnology to remove contaminants and ensure that the water is safe for reuse. Additionally, bioreactors can be integrated into these systems, leveraging microbial processes to break down organic waste and convert it into usable water. This closed-loop system will minimise water loss and reduce the need for external water sourcing, a vital consideration in space habitats where resources are limited.

In conjunction with recycling efforts, water conservation strategies will also play an essential role. Implementing smart irrigation techniques for extraterrestrial agriculture will be key to optimising water usage. Technologies such as drip irrigation and moisture sensors can be employed to ensure that plants receive only the necessary amount of water, minimising waste. Further, selecting drought-resistant genetically modified crops will enhance agricultural sustainability, ensuring that food production aligns with water conservation efforts in harsh environments.

Another significant aspect of water management in space habitats will be the design of biodomes and ecosystems that naturally recycle water. By creating closed ecological systems, water can be cycled between various components of the habitat, such as plants, animals, and microorganisms. Rainwater collection systems and fog nets can also be utilised to capture moisture from the atmosphere, augmenting water supplies. Careful planning in the design of these biodomes will ensure that they function efficiently, mimicking Earth's hydrological cycles while adapting to the unique conditions of other planets.

As we advance toward a future of off-world colonies, the ethical considerations surrounding water management must also be addressed. Policies governing the allocation and use of water resources will need to be established, ensuring equitable access for all inhabitants of extraterrestrial environments. Education and public awareness campaigns will be vital in promoting water conservation practices among settlers, fostering a culture of sustainability from the outset. By prioritising water recycling and conservation strategies, we can create resilient and thriving ecosystems that support human life on other planets, paving the way for a sustainable future in the cosmos.

Chapter 13: Energy generation systems for sustainable living on other planets

Solar Power in space

Solar power serves as a crucial component in the quest for sustainable energy solutions for extraterrestrial habitats. Harnessing solar energy in space presents unique advantages due to the absence of atmospheric interference and the constant availability of sunlight in certain regions. Unlike earth, where weather patterns can obstruct solar energy collection, space environments, particularly those in close proximity to the Sun, can utilise solar panels to their maximum potential. This reliability makes solar power an ideal candidate for energy generation systems in off-world colonies, where consistent energy supply is essential for survival and development.

The design and implementation of solar power systems in space require careful consideration of the unique challenges posed by extraterrestrial environments. Solar panels must be engineered to withstand extreme temperature fluctuations, radiation exposure, and micrometeoroid impacts. Advanced materials and technologies are being developed to enhance the durability and efficiency of solar arrays. Moreover, the ability to deploy solar panels on the surfaces of other planets or moons, or even in orbit, can significantly impact energy generation capabilities. These systems must also be integrated with energy storage solutions to ensure a stable power supply during periods of darkness or increased energy demand.

In terms of terrestrial terraforming, solar power plays a vital role in supporting soil enhancement methods for extraterrestrial agriculture. By providing the necessary energy to power hydroponic systems, nutrient delivery mechanisms, and other agricultural technologies, solar energy enables the cultivation of crops in previously inhospitable environments. The use of genetically modified plants that can thrive under low-light conditions or with minimal resources can further enhance agricultural productivity. By ensuring a reliable energy source, solar power can help establish self-sustaining ecosystems that are crucial for long-term habitation.

Water sourcing and management in space habitats can also benefit from solar power. Energy generated from solar panels can be used to drive processes such as electrolysis for water extraction from lunar regolith or Martian soil. Additionally, solar energy can power water purification systems, ensuring a clean and sustainable water supply for off-world inhabitants. Efficient water management systems that utilise solar energy will be essential for maintaining the health and well-being of colonists, as well as for supporting agricultural initiatives necessary for survival.

The integration of solar power into biodome design and ecosystem management is another critical aspect of establishing off-world colonies. Solar energy can be harnessed to regulate temperature, humidity, and ventilation within biodomes, creating optimal conditions for both human habitation and plant growth. By employing innovative energy generation systems, habitats can be designed to be self-sufficient and resilient. As we move toward 2099, understanding the intricacies of solar power in space will be fundamental in shaping the policies, ethics, and frameworks that guide the terraforming and colonisation of other worlds, ensuring that these endeavours are sustainable and equitable for all.

Nuclear energy applications

Nuclear energy has emerged as a cornerstone technology for the ambitious goals of terraforming and establishing sustainable habitats on other planets by 2099. Its potential applications span various critical areas, including energy generation, water management, and agricultural enhancement, all of which are vital for supporting human life in extraterrestrial environments. Given the limitations of solar and wind energy in the harsh conditions of space, nuclear power stands out as a reliable and efficient alternative capable of delivering consistent energy output necessary for long-term missions and colony development.

Finally, the ethical considerations surrounding the use of nuclear energy in terraforming are paramount. Policymakers must ensure that nuclear technologies are developed and deployed responsibly, with stringent safety measures to protect both human settlers and the extraterrestrial environments they inhabit. Establishing international frameworks for nuclear energy governance will be essential in addressing potential risks, such as contamination or proliferation, while enabling the benefits of this powerful energy source to be realised in the quest for sustainable off-world living. By balancing innovation with ethical responsibility, we can pave the way for successful terraforming initiatives that empower humanity to thrive beyond earth.

Alternative Energy Sources and Innovations

Alternative energy sources and innovations are essential components in the quest for sustainable living on other planets, particularly as humanity prepares for the challenges of terraforming and colonising extraterrestrial environments by 2099. Conventional energy sources such as fossil fuels are not viable in space; thus, innovative alternatives must be explored and refined. Solar energy, already the most abundant resource in our solar system, will play a pivotal role in powering habitats and supporting agriculture on other worlds. Advanced solar panels and concentrated solar power systems can be adapted to maximise efficiency even in less-than-ideal sunlight conditions, making them critical for energy generation in various extraterrestrial locales.

In addition to solar energy, other renewable sources such as wind and geothermal energy offer promising alternatives for off-world colonies. While traditional wind energy harnessing may be limited on planets with sparse atmospheres, innovative designs can capture even the slightest breezes. Geothermal energy, available on planets with volcanic activity, presents another viable option. By leveraging the natural heat beneath the surface, energy systems can be designed to provide consistent power for habitats, agricultural systems, and life support technologies, reducing dependence on energy imports from earth.

Innovative battery storage solutions and energy management systems will be necessary to integrate these energy sources effectively. Energy storage technologies, such as advanced lithium-sulfur batteries or solid-state batteries, provide the capability to store renewable energy for use during periods of low production. Smart grid systems will also be essential for optimising energy use across various habitats, ensuring that energy is distributed efficiently to support daily activities and agricultural operations. These systems will enable energy independence for extraterrestrial colonies, fostering self-sufficiency and resilience.

In the context of terraforming, energy innovations will also drive advancements in soil enhancement and water management techniques. For instance, energy-efficient desalination methods, powered by renewable sources, can ensure that water is readily available for both drinking and irrigation in extraterrestrial agricultural systems. Furthermore, energy-driven technologies can assist in soil amendment processes, allowing for the introduction of essential nutrients and microorganisms needed to create fertile ground capable of supporting genetically modified crops designed for alien environments.

Finally, the integration of alternative energy systems into biodome designs and ecosystem management strategies will be crucial for the success of off-world colonies. Efficient energy use not only supports habitat construction and maintenance but also ensures that ecosystems within these biodomes can thrive. By harnessing renewable energy to power artificial lighting, temperature control, and water recycling systems, colonies can create sustainable environments that mimic earth's ecosystems, thereby enhancing the prospects for human health and well-being in long-term space habitation. As humanity looks toward the stars, embracing these innovative energy solutions will be fundamental to realising the dream of creating habitable worlds by the end of the century.

Chapter 14: Biodome design and ecosystem management for off-world colonies

Design principles for biodomes

Designing biodomes for extraterrestrial habitats requires a comprehensive understanding of various principles that ensure their functionality, sustainability, and adaptability to alien environments. The primary design principle focuses on creating a self-sustaining ecosystem that can support human life while accommodating the unique challenges presented by the off-world environment. This includes considerations for atmospheric composition, temperature regulation, and radiation protection, which are critical for the survival of both humans and plants. The biodome must replicate and optimize earth-like conditions, such as humidity and pressure, while being resilient to external factors such as meteorite impacts or solar flares.

Another vital principle is the integration of advanced agricultural techniques within the biodome. Soil enhancement methods must be designed to thrive in extraterrestrial conditions, possibly utilising hydroponics, aeroponics, or even soil-less agriculture to maximize crop yield. Genetic modification of plants can play a pivotal role in this aspect, allowing for the cultivation of crops that can withstand harsh conditions, such as varying gravity levels and lower light availability. By engineering plants to be more resilient and productive, biodomes can become a reliable source of food, reducing dependency on supply missions from earth.

Water sourcing and management is another critical aspect of biodome design. Efficient systems for recycling and purifying water are essential, as water resources will be limited in extraterrestrial environments. Implementing closed-loop systems that capture evapotranspiration from plants and recycle wastewater will help maintain a stable water supply. Additionally, exploring the utilisation of local water sources, such as ice deposits on planets like Mars, could supplement the biodome's water needs. This principle emphasises the importance of resource efficiency and conservation in maintaining a sustainable habitat.

Energy generation systems must also be integrated into the biodome's design. Renewable energy sources, such as solar power and wind energy, can be harnessed to provide a continuous energy supply for life support systems, lighting, and agricultural operations. The biodome should be equipped with energy storage solutions to ensure a stable energy supply during periods of low generation, like during dust storms on Mars. By designing a biodome that prioritises energy efficiency and sustainability, we can create a living environment that minimises its ecological footprint while maximising productivity.

Lastly, ecosystem management is essential for maintaining the health and balance of the biodome's environment. This involves monitoring plant growth, pest control, and the overall health of the ecosystem to ensure it remains stable and productive over time. Utilising advanced technologies such as artificial intelligence can facilitate the management of these systems, allowing for real-time adjustments and interventions as needed. By adhering to these design principles, biodomes can become effective habitats that support human life and foster a thriving ecosystem, paving the way for successful terrestrial terraforming and sustainable living on other planets by 2099.

Creating sustainable ecosystems

Creating sustainable ecosystems in extraterrestrial environments is a critical aspect of successful terraforming efforts aimed at establishing habitable worlds by 2099. The foundation of these ecosystems lies in understanding the unique challenges posed by alien terrains, climates, and atmospheric conditions. To facilitate life, it is essential to replicate earth-like conditions as closely as possible, while also incorporating innovative techniques tailored for specific extraterrestrial circumstances. This requires a multidisciplinary approach that combines environmental science, engineering, and biology to create a balanced ecosystem that can thrive in harsh environments.

Soil enhancement methods are paramount to ensuring agricultural sustainability on other planets. Techniques such as bioaugmentation, where beneficial microbes are introduced to improve soil fertility, can be employed to bolster nutrient availability. Additionally, the use of hydroponic and aeroponic systems may allow for efficient food production without the need for traditional soil, making them ideal solutions for environments with less-than-ideal terrestrial soil conditions. Incorporating organic waste recycling into these systems will further enhance soil quality and contribute to a circular economy that minimises waste while maximising resource utilisation.

Chapter 15: Genetic modification of plants for alien environments

Understanding genetic engineering

Genetic engineering, a cornerstone of modern biotechnology, holds immense potential for transforming agriculture and ecology in the context of extraterrestrial habitats. As we venture into the cosmos, the necessity to adapt terrestrial life forms to alien environments becomes paramount. By modifying the genetic makeup of plants and organisms, we can create resilient species capable of thriving in the harsh conditions found on other planets. These engineered organisms can be designed to tolerate extreme temperatures, radiation, and nutrient-deficient soils, essential factors for successful terraforming efforts.

One of the primary applications of genetic engineering in extraterrestrial agriculture is the enhancement of soil quality and plant growth. For instance, soil on Mars and other celestial bodies lacks many essential nutrients and has high salinity levels. Through genetic modification, we can develop plant varieties that possess traits such as increased root efficiency, enhanced nutrient uptake, and the ability to process saline water. This adaptation not only improves the likelihood of successful crop yields but also contributes to soil enhancement methods that are vital for sustainable agriculture in space.

.

Plant adaptation strategies

Plant adaptation strategies are crucial for the successful establishment of sustainable ecosystems in extraterrestrial environments. As we venture into the process of terraforming and creating habitable worlds by 2099, understanding how plants can be modified and cultivated to thrive in alien conditions will play a pivotal role in ensuring food security and ecological balance. This subchapter examines various strategies that could be employed to adapt terrestrial plants for the unique challenges posed by other planets.

One of the primary strategies involves genetic modification, which allows scientists to enhance specific traits in plants that are vital for survival in harsh environments. For instance, altering the genetic makeup of crops can improve their tolerance to extreme temperatures, increased radiation, and variations in soil composition that are likely to occur on other planets. This could involve the introduction of genes responsible for drought resistance or the ability to utilize nutrients more efficiently. As genetic engineering technologies advance, the potential for creating resilient plant varieties that can flourish in extraterrestrial habitats becomes increasingly feasible.

Another essential adaptation strategy is the development of soil enhancement methods tailored for extraterrestrial agriculture. The regolith found on planets like Mars, for example, is not inherently fertile and lacks the organic matter necessary for plant growth. By using techniques such as bioaugmentation, where beneficial microbes are introduced to improve soil health, or by integrating organic waste recycling systems, we can create a more hospitable growing medium. These methods will not only support plant life but also contribute to the overall sustainability of the ecosystem, as they promote nutrient cycling and soil structure improvement.

In summary, the evolution of plant adaptation strategies will be fundamental to the success of terraforming efforts and the establishment of self-sustaining colonies on other planets. By leveraging advancements in genetic engineering, soil management, water conservation, and ecosystem design, we can create robust agricultural systems capable of supporting human life in extraterrestrial environments. This ongoing research and innovation will not only facilitate off-world agriculture but also provide valuable insights into sustainable practices that can be applied on Earth, demonstrating the interconnectedness of our planetary challenges and solutions.

Ethical considerations in genetic modification

Ethical considerations in genetic modification are crucial as humanity ventures into the realm of terraforming and establishing sustainable life in extraterrestrial environments. As scientists and engineers explore the genetic alteration of plants and organisms to thrive in unfamiliar conditions, it is essential to address the moral implications of such advancements. The potential benefits of genetically modified organisms (GMOs) include improved resilience to harsh climates, enhanced nutrient profiles, and greater efficiency in resource use, which are paramount for agriculture in space habitats. However, these benefits are accompanied by concerns about ecological balance, unforeseen consequences, and the long-term effects on both modified species and their native counterparts.

One significant ethical concern surrounding genetic modification is the potential for unintended ecological disruptions. When introducing genetically modified plants into alien ecosystems, there exists a risk that these organisms could outcompete native species or disrupt existing food webs. The introduction of GMOs may lead to reduced biodiversity, which is essential for ecosystem stability. Therefore, rigorous testing and monitoring must be in place to ensure that the ecological impact of these modifications is thoroughly understood before they are deployed in terraforming efforts.

Moreover, the modification process itself raises questions about the integrity of natural organisms. Genetic modification can be seen as an overreach of human intervention, potentially leading to a slippery slope where the boundaries of ethical science are blurred. As we design plants to survive the conditions of Mars or other celestial bodies, we must consider the implications of creating life forms that do not exist in nature. The philosophical debate surrounding the "right" to alter life forms for human benefit must be engaged, emphasising the need for transparency and public discourse on these issues.

Another layer of ethical consideration involves the ownership and control of genetically modified organisms. As corporations and governments invest in genetic engineering for space agriculture, issues of patenting and intellectual property emerge. This could lead to monopolies on essential food sources, limiting access for certain populations and exacerbating existing inequalities. Establishing fair policies and frameworks for the distribution and use of GMOs in extraterrestrial environments is necessary to promote equity and justice in the burgeoning field of space colonisation.

Lastly, the ethical considerations in genetic modification extend to the health implications for humans who will inhabit these new worlds. As we genetically enhance plants for better growth and sustainability, it is crucial to assess the safety of consuming these modified organisms. Long-term health effects must be studied to avoid potential risks to human health in off-world colonies. A comprehensive ethical framework that prioritises safety, equity, and ecological integrity will be vital in guiding the responsible use of genetic modification as humanity embarks on the journey of terraforming tomorrow.

Chapter 16: Construction materials and methods for extraterrestrial structures

Materials suitable for space construction

Materials suitable for space construction must meet a range of stringent criteria, including lightweight properties, durability, resistance to radiation, and thermal stability. Advances in materials science have led to the exploration of various substances that can be utilised in extraterrestrial environments. These materials not only need to withstand harsh conditions but also ideally should be locally sourced to reduce the logistical burden of transporting construction materials from earth. Innovations in this field could play a pivotal role in establishing sustainable habitats on other planets.

One promising category of materials is in-situ resource utilisation (ISRU) materials. This involves using local resources to create building materials, such as regolith, which is the layer of loose, fragmented material covering solid bedrock on celestial bodies like the Moon and Mars. Techniques such as sintering or 3D printing can transform regolith into bricks or other structural forms. This approach not only minimises the need for earth-based materials but also fosters self-sufficiency in off-world colonies, allowing for expansion and adaptation as needs evolve.

Another area of interest is advanced composites, including carbon fiber and polymer-based materials. These composites are known for their high strength-to-weight ratios and resistance to environmental degradation. They can be engineered to provide exceptional insulation against extreme temperatures and radiation, crucial for the safety of inhabitants. Additionally, these materials can be tailored to incorporate smart technologies that monitor structural integrity and environmental conditions, enhancing the resilience of habitats in space.

Metals such as titanium and aluminum alloys also hold significant potential for space construction. Their lightweight nature combined with strength makes them ideal for frameworks and structural supports. These metals can be treated to improve their resistance to corrosion and temperature fluctuations, which are essential properties for maintaining the safety and longevity of structures in extraterrestrial environments. Moreover, the ability to recycle and repurpose these metals from decommissioned equipment or failed structures further enhances their sustainability.

Ultimately, the development of materials for space construction is not just about the physical properties but also about the ethical implications of colonisation. As we venture into the cosmos, it is vital to consider the impact of our construction practices on potential extraterrestrial ecosystems. The choice of construction materials should reflect a commitment to minimising our footprint while fostering the growth of sustainable, habitable environments. This holistic approach will ensure that the materials we select contribute positively to the broader goals of terraforming and creating thriving off-world communities.

Innovative building techniques

Innovative building techniques are essential for establishing sustainable habitats on other planets, particularly as humanity seeks to expand its presence beyond earth. As we approach 2099, advancements in construction methods will play a pivotal role in designing and erecting structures that can withstand the unique challenges posed by extraterrestrial environments. These techniques will not only focus on the durability and resilience of buildings but also on their integration with the surrounding ecosystems, ensuring that off-world colonies can thrive in harmony with their artificial environments.

Biomimicry is another innovative approach gaining traction in the realm of extraterrestrial construction. By studying and emulating natural processes and structures found on earth, architects and engineers can devise solutions that are both efficient and sustainable. For example, designs inspired by termite mounds, which regulate temperature and humidity effectively, could inform the construction of energy-efficient habitats. Such designs would not only enhance the livability of these structures but also minimise the energy required for climate control, leading to more sustainable living conditions.

Finally, the integration of smart technologies into building designs will revolutionise how habitats are managed and maintained. Utilising sensors and IoT devices, structures can adapt to changing environmental conditions in real-time, optimising energy use and ensuring resource management is both efficient and sustainable. This intelligent infrastructure will facilitate advanced water sourcing and management systems, energy generation, and even agricultural practices within off-world colonies, ultimately supporting the long-term health and well-being of inhabitants. As we advance toward 2099, the fusion of these innovative building techniques will be crucial for creating successful and sustainable extraterrestrial habitats.

3D printing in space construction

3D printing technology is revolutionising the construction of habitats in space, offering innovative solutions to the unique challenges posed by extraterrestrial environments. As humanity looks to establish permanent settlements on other planets, the need for efficient, sustainable building methods becomes paramount. Traditional construction techniques are often impractical in space due to factors such as limited resources, microgravity, and the harsh conditions of celestial bodies. 3D printing allows for the utilisation of local materials, significantly reducing the need to transport building supplies from earth. This capability aligns perfectly with the goals of terrestrial terraforming and the establishment of viable ecosystems in off-world colonies.

One of the most promising aspects of 3D printing in space construction is its ability to create structures using in-situ resources, such as regolith found on the Moon and Mars. By employing techniques such as sintering or binding, 3D printers can transform these materials into durable building components. This not only minimises the logistical challenges associated with transporting materials but also promotes a self-sustaining approach to construction. The use of local materials fosters a deeper connection with the environment of the new world, paving the way for more natural integration of human habitats with extraterrestrial landscapes.

The design of biodomes and living spaces for off-world colonies greatly benefits from the flexibility of 3D printing technology. Architects and engineers can utilise advanced software to create complex structures tailored to the specific needs of their inhabitants. This adaptability is crucial for addressing the varying conditions on different planets, such as temperature fluctuations, radiation exposure, and atmospheric composition. Customised designs can incorporate features such as integrated energy systems and water management solutions, enhancing the overall sustainability of space habitats. Furthermore, 3D printing allows for rapid prototyping, enabling iterative design processes that can quickly respond to new findings and challenges encountered during colonisation efforts.

In addition to structural applications, 3D printing holds potential for creating essential components for life support systems, including water filtration systems and energy generation devices. As off-world colonies develop, ensuring a reliable supply of clean water and sustainable energy becomes critical. Innovative 3D-printed solutions can include efficient solar panel structures or components for bioreactors that recycle waste into usable resources. This integration of technology not only supports the health and well-being of colonists but also aligns with ethical frameworks guiding terraforming initiatives, ensuring that human activities do not harm potential alien ecosystems.

As we advance toward the goal of creating habitable worlds by 2099, the role of 3D printing in space construction becomes a necessary tool. Its ability to leverage local materials, facilitate complex designs, and produce essential life support components positions it as a cornerstone of off-world development. As we continue to explore and settle new planets, the innovative use of 3D printing will play a crucial role in shaping sustainable, resilient habitats that can support human life, ultimately paving the way for a thriving presence beyond earth.

Chapter 17: Terraforming ethics and policy frameworks

Ethical considerations in terraforming

Ethical considerations in terraforming extend beyond the technical challenges of transforming other planets into habitable environments. These considerations encompass the moral responsibilities humanity holds towards extraterrestrial ecosystems, potential indigenous life forms, and the long-term consequences of altering an entire planet. As we advance towards the goal of terraforming by 2099, we must critically examine the implications of our actions and develop frameworks that prioritise ethical decision-making in this unprecedented endeavour. The idea is to try and refrain from space-construction that might disrupt, change or alter anything without serious reasons especially if there might be life-forms or important microstructures that humans might interfere with.

This is actually one of the primary ethical concerns in terraforming is the potential disruption of existing ecosystems, even in the absence of known life forms. The introduction of earth-based species for agriculture, such as genetically modified plants designed to thrive in alien soils, raises questions about the integrity of these environments. It is essential to evaluate the impact of such modifications not only on the target environment but also on earth's ecosystems, which could be affected by the unintended consequences of our interventions. Responsible stewardship of other worlds requires a commitment to minimising harm and preserving the natural state of these celestial bodies.

Another critical aspect of terraforming ethics involves the implications for potential extraterrestrial life. If life exists on a target planet, even in microbial forms, the act of terraforming could be considered an invasion or colonisation of that environment which indeed it is. Ethical frameworks must prioritise the respect for life, encompassing the principle of non-maleficence, which advocates for avoiding harm to existing organisms. Policymakers and scientists need to ensure that any terraforming project is preceded by thorough exploration and study of the planet's biological landscape to understand and protect any indigenous life forms that might exist.

In addition to ecological concerns, the ethical dimensions of terraforming also intersect with issues of governance, equity, and social justice. As humanity embarks on the journey of creating habitable worlds, questions arise about who gets to decide how these new environments are shaped and who benefits from the resources they offer. It is crucial to establish inclusive policies that involve diverse stakeholders, ensuring that the voices of marginalised communities are heard in discussions about extraterrestrial colonisation. The equitable distribution of resources and opportunities in off-world habitats must be a priority, preventing the emergence of new forms of inequality that could arise in the pursuit of terraforming.

Lastly, the long-term sustainability of terraformed environments poses ethical dilemmas regarding our responsibilities to future generations. The energy generation systems and soil enhancement methods we implement must consider not only present needs but also the lasting impact these technologies will have on the new worlds we create. Ethical terraforming practices should integrate principles of sustainability, ensuring that off-world colonies can thrive without exhausting their resources or compromising their ecosystems. This forward-thinking approach will help foster a harmonious coexistence with the environments we transform, balancing human aspirations with the health and integrity of other planets.

International policies and agreements

International policies and agreements play a crucial role in shaping the future of terrestrial terraforming and the establishment of habitable worlds beyond earth. As humanity looks toward the stars, various nations and organisations must collaborate to ensure that these ambitious projects are conducted responsibly and ethically. The United Nations Office for Outer Space Affairs (UNOOSA) has been at the forefront of promoting international cooperation in the exploration and use of outer space. Their guidelines emphasise the need for sustainable practices and the preservation of celestial bodies, which is essential as we develop methods for terraforming and establishing off-world colonies.

The Outer Space Treaty of 1967 serves as the foundation for many international agreements relating to space activities. This treaty stipulates that space exploration should benefit all humankind and prohibits the appropriation of outer space by any one nation. As terraforming technologies advance, countries must work together to interpret and adapt this treaty to encompass the emerging challenges associated with creating habitable environments on other planets. The principles outlined in the treaty will be instrumental in guiding policies surrounding extraterrestrial agriculture, water sourcing, and energy generation systems, ensuring these endeavours are equitable and inclusive.

In addition to the Outer Space Treaty, various international frameworks are emerging to address the ethical implications of terraforming and colonisation. The concept of planetary protection, which aims to prevent biological contamination of other celestial bodies and protect earth's biosphere, is gaining traction. As genetic modification of plants and other organisms becomes integral to adapting life for alien environments, policies must be established to regulate these practices. International agreements should facilitate the sharing of knowledge and technology while ensuring that ethical considerations are prioritised, particularly concerning the potential impacts on existing extraterrestrial ecosystems.

Finally, as humanity embarks on this unprecedented journey, the establishment of a global governance framework for terraforming initiatives is essential. This framework should incorporate diverse perspectives from various stakeholders, including scientists, ethicists, policymakers, and the public. By fostering open dialogue and collaboration, international policies can ensure that terraforming projects are not only scientifically sound but also socially responsible. The successful colonisation of other planets will depend on our ability to navigate the complex interplay of technology, ethics, and international cooperation, ultimately paving the way for a sustainable and harmonious existence beyond Earth.

Public engagement and opinion

Public engagement and opinion play a crucial role in the development and implementation of terraforming projects aimed at creating habitable worlds by 2099. As humanity stands on the brink of a new era in space exploration, the need for transparent communication and active participation from the public is very necessary. Engaging diverse communities in discussions about terraforming initiatives not only fosters a sense of ownership and responsibility but also ensures that various perspectives and concerns are addressed. This engagement can take many forms, from public forums and workshops to social media campaigns and collaborative research projects, all aimed at demystifying complex scientific concepts and encouraging informed debate.

One of the primary areas of public concern relates to the environmental implications of terraforming efforts. Citizens are increasingly aware of the ecological challenges faced on earth, such as climate change and habitat destruction. As such, it is essential to communicate the benefits and risks associated with soil enhancement methods for extraterrestrial agriculture, water sourcing and management, and energy generation systems. By educating the public on sustainable practices that can be employed in off-world environments, such as the use of genetically modified plants tailored for alien conditions, we can build trust and support for these initiatives. Moreover, providing clear information about how these methods can mitigate potential adverse effects on extraterrestrial ecosystems is vital for fostering public acceptance.

The ethical dimensions of terraforming also warrant thorough public discourse. The question of whether it is right to alter another planet's environment to suit human needs is a complex one that must be navigated carefully. Engaging the public in discussions about terraforming ethics and policy frameworks can help formulate guidelines that reflect societal values and priorities. By including diverse voices in these conversations, we can work towards a consensus that respects both human aspirations and the integrity of extraterrestrial ecosystems. This dialogue is essential not only for the development of ethical standards but also for instilling a sense of responsibility among future generations of space explorers.

In addition to environmental and ethical considerations, health and medical innovations for long-term space habitation are paramount topics that require public attention. The challenges of sustaining human life in extraterrestrial environments, including the psychological and physiological impacts of isolation and altered gravity, must be openly discussed. By fostering a community of interest around these issues, we can encourage collaborative efforts between scientists, healthcare professionals, and the public to develop effective solutions. Public engagement initiatives could include informational campaigns that highlight ongoing research and innovations in this domain, thereby inspiring confidence in the feasibility of long-term off-world living.

Ultimately, creating a collaborative framework for public engagement in terraforming projects will enhance the likelihood of success for these ambitious endeavours. By prioritising transparency, fostering open dialogue, and actively involving communities in the decision-making process, we can cultivate a sense of shared purpose and commitment to the future of humanity in space. As we work to transform distant worlds into habitable environments, the collective input and support of the public will be instrumental in shaping a future that aligns with both scientific progress and ethical responsibility.

Chapter 18: Health and medical innovations for long-term space habitation

Health risks in space environments

Health risks in space environments pose significant challenges for human survival and well-being during long-term missions and colonisation efforts on other planets. The unique conditions of space, including microgravity, radiation exposure, and confined living quarters, can lead to a range of health issues that must be addressed to ensure the success of terraforming initiatives. Understanding these risks is essential for developing effective strategies to mitigate them and promote the health of future space inhabitants.

One of the primary health concerns in space is the detrimental effect of microgravity on the human body. Prolonged exposure to microgravity can lead to muscle atrophy and bone density loss, making astronauts more susceptible to fractures and injuries. Research has shown that astronauts can lose up to 20% of their muscle mass and 1-2% of their bone density per month in space. To combat these effects, it is crucial to implement robust exercise regimens and resistance training protocols within space habitats, ensuring that inhabitants maintain their physical health and strength during extended missions.

Radiation exposure is another significant health risk in space environments, as cosmic rays and solar radiation can damage DNA and increase the likelihood of cancer and other illnesses. Unlike earth, which has a protective atmosphere and magnetic field, space exposes individuals to higher levels of radiation. Effective shielding strategies, such as incorporating radiation-resistant materials in habitat construction and designing structures with optimal orientation, are essential. Additionally, monitoring radiation levels and developing medical countermeasures to address potential health impacts will be vital for the safety of off-world colonies.

Mental health is also a critical factor in the health risks associated with space habitation. The psychological challenges of isolation, confinement, and the absence of familiar social interactions can lead to stress, anxiety, and depression among space inhabitants. To mitigate these risks, it is important to create living environments that foster community and social interaction, as well as provide access to recreational activities and mental health support. Furthermore, ongoing research into the psychological impacts of long-duration spaceflight will inform best practices for maintaining mental well-being in extraterrestrial settings.

Finally, the management of health care in space environments is an essential consideration for long-term habitation. Limited access to medical facilities and resources necessitates the development of innovative health care solutions, including telemedicine, advanced diagnostics, and portable medical technologies. Training crew members in basic medical procedures and establishing protocols for emergency situations are crucial in ensuring that health risks can be effectively managed. As we move towards the goal of terraforming and sustaining human life on other planets, addressing these health risks will be paramount in creating viable and thriving off-world communities.

Medical technologies for space colonies

Medical technologies play a crucial role in ensuring the health and well-being of inhabitants in space colonies. As we envision the establishment of permanent human settlements beyond earth, it is essential to develop sophisticated healthcare systems capable of addressing the unique challenges posed by extraterrestrial environments. These challenges include exposure to cosmic radiation, microgravity effects, and the psychological strains of living in isolated and confined spaces. Advanced medical technologies will not only provide immediate care but will also focus on preventive measures to maintain the health of colonists over extended periods.

Telemedicine will be a cornerstone of healthcare in space colonies, enabling remote consultations and diagnosis. With a vast distance between earth and colonies, immediate access to terrestrial medical experts may be limited. Telemedicine platforms will facilitate real-time communication between astronauts and healthcare providers on earth, allowing for expert advice and treatment plans without the need for physical presence. By utilising advanced imaging technologies and wearable health monitoring devices, medical professionals can assess the health conditions of colonists, making it possible to provide timely interventions even in the absence of specialists on-site.

In addition to telemedicine, biotechnology will revolutionise medical treatments in space. Genetic engineering and synthetic biology will enable the development of tailored therapies that address the specific health risks associated with extraterrestrial living. For example, the use of genetically modified organisms could lead to the creation of crops that are not only nutritious but also produce compounds that enhance human health, such as vitamins and pharmaceuticals. Furthermore, bioreactors could be employed to synthesise drugs on-demand, reducing the need for extensive pharmaceutical supplies transported from earth.

Robotic and automated systems will also play an integral role in delivering healthcare services in space. Surgical robots equipped with advanced precision tools can perform complex procedures under the guidance of earth-based surgeons. These systems will be essential for addressing medical emergencies on colonies where immediate evacuation may not be feasible. Additionally, autonomous drones could be equipped with medical supplies and deliver them to remote locations within the colony, ensuring that essential resources are always within reach.

The psychological well-being of colonists is as important as their physical health. Mental health technologies, including virtual reality environments designed for relaxation and social interaction, will be essential in combating isolation and stress. Furthermore, ongoing psychological assessments will help identify individuals at risk of mental health crises, allowing for early intervention. By integrating these medical technologies into the fabric of space colonies, we can create robust healthcare systems that not only sustain human life but also promote a thriving and resilient community in the cosmos.

Finally, ongoing research into the psychological impacts of isolation will be crucial as humanity embarks on long-duration space missions. Understanding how different individuals react to confinement and limited social interaction will inform best practices for maintaining mental health. By prioritising psychological well-being in the design and management of extraterrestrial habitats, we can ensure that colonisers are not only physically equipped to terraform new worlds but also mentally prepared to thrive in these challenging environments.

Chapter 19: Future prospects and challenges in terraforming

Anticipated technological advances

Anticipated technological advances in terraforming by 2099 will significantly reshape our approach to creating habitable worlds beyond earth. One of the foremost areas of development will be in soil enhancement methods tailored for extraterrestrial agriculture. As we venture to Mars or the moons of Jupiter and Saturn, the native soil will often be inhospitable for traditional farming. Researchers are expected to design bioengineered microbes and nutrient-rich additives that can transform barren soil into fertile ground, allowing for the cultivation of crops necessary for sustaining human life. This will not only provide food but also contribute to the atmospheric processes essential for long-term terraforming efforts.

Water sourcing and management will be another critical focus area. Innovative technologies such as advanced atmospheric water generators and ice mining robots will likely be deployed to extract water from the environment, whether from polar ice caps on Mars or subsurface aquifers on Europa. Effective water recycling systems will also be developed to ensure that water is continuously purified and reused within habitats. By establishing a reliable water supply, we can support agriculture, drinking needs, and even hydroponic systems, which will be essential for sustaining human life in off-world colonies.

Energy generation systems will undergo transformative changes, with a strong emphasis on sustainability. By 2099, solar power technology is expected to have advanced significantly, with large-scale solar farms capable of harnessing energy not only from the sun but also from other celestial bodies. Fusion energy, previously a theoretical concept, may become a feasible solution, providing a near-limitless power source. These advancements will be crucial for powering habitats, agricultural facilities, and technologies necessary for terraforming processes. The development of energy storage systems, such as advanced batteries or supercapacitors, will also ensure a stable energy supply during periods of low generation.

Biodome design and ecosystem management will be vital for establishing stable environments for human habitation. Future biodomes will likely utilise smart materials that adapt to environmental changes, providing optimal conditions for plant growth and human comfort. These structures will be integrated with automated systems for monitoring air quality, temperature, and humidity, ensuring a balanced ecosystem. Additionally, innovations in genetic modification will enable the creation of plants that can thrive in alien environments, contributing to the biodiversity necessary for a self-sustaining ecosystem.

As we embrace these technological advances, ethical considerations and policy frameworks will need to evolve alongside them. The complexities of terraforming raise important questions about the preservation of native ecosystems and the rights of potential extraterrestrial life forms. By 2099, it will be essential to establish international agreements and ethical guidelines governing terraforming practices, ensuring that our endeavors do not lead to irreversible harm. Continuous dialogue among scientists, ethicists, and policymakers will be necessary to navigate these challenges, fostering a responsible approach to creating new worlds for human habitation.

Overcoming economic and political hurdles

Overcoming economic and political hurdles is crucial for the successful implementation of terrestrial terraforming projects aimed at creating habitable worlds by 2099. As nations and private entities invest in space colonisation, it is essential to navigate the complex landscape of economic constraints and political dynamics that can impede progress. Funding remains one of the most significant challenges. Large-scale terraforming initiatives require substantial financial resources, often necessitating public-private partnerships. Governments must recognise the long-term benefits of investing in these projects, while companies must be willing to share the risks associated with pioneering new technologies and approaches.

Political support is equally vital. Legislation and international treaties will play critical roles in shaping the policies that govern terraforming efforts. The establishment of clear frameworks can help mitigate conflicts over resource allocation and environmental protection. Engaging in dialogue with stakeholders, including environmental groups, scientific communities, and the public, can foster a collaborative atmosphere. This cooperation is essential for addressing concerns about the ethical implications of altering extraterrestrial environments and ensuring that terraforming practices do not harm existing ecosystems or violate principles of planetary protection.

Another significant hurdle is the management of resources, particularly in the context of water sourcing and energy generation for sustainable living in off-world colonies. Efficient water management systems must be developed to address the scarcity of this vital resource on other planets. Innovative methods for capturing and recycling water, alongside advanced energy generation systems, will be necessary to support colonisation efforts. Developing these systems requires investment in research and technology, which can be hindered by economic limitations. Thus, fostering a robust economy that prioritises these initiatives is essential for overcoming such challenges.

Soil enhancement methods for extraterrestrial agriculture also present unique obstacles. The composition of Martian or lunar soil may not support traditional farming techniques, necessitating research into genetic modification of plants and the use of innovative growth mediums. Economic support for agricultural research and development can lead to breakthroughs that enhance food security for off-world colonies. Addressing these scientific challenges through strategic funding and collaboration can pave the way for successful agricultural practices that ensure the survival of human populations in space.

Lastly, the design of biodomes and the management of ecosystems will require interdisciplinary approaches that integrate engineering, biology, and environmental science. These efforts will need to be supported by policies that promote responsible management of both terrestrial and extraterrestrial resources. By addressing economic and political hurdles through strategic collaboration, innovative research, and comprehensive policy frameworks, humanity can lay the groundwork for sustainable and ethical terraforming initiatives that will make creating habitable worlds a reality by 2099.

Envisioning life on other worlds by 2099

Envisioning life on other worlds by 2099 requires a comprehensive understanding of the various elements that will contribute to the feasibility of human habitation beyond earth. The ambitious goal of terraforming planets like Mars or moons such as Europa hinges on advancements in soil enhancement methods that will enable sustainable agriculture in extraterrestrial environments. By the end of the century, scientists anticipate the development of synthetic soils enriched with essential nutrients and microorganisms tailored to thrive in alien conditions. These innovations will not only support crop growth but will also establish a vital ecosystem that mimics earth's agricultural systems, ensuring food security for colonists.

For everything we do, there is always a need for water and we have plenty of it on the planet earth, as for this commondity availability in othern planetory systems, it becomes a matter of being able to manufucture, formulate or extract it be it connate water or other forms of combination of substances when living off-earth. Hence water sourcing and management will be critical components of life on other worlds. As we look to 2099, it is projected that advanced technologies for extracting water from sub-surface ice or utilising atmospheric moisture will be commonplace. Systems designed for efficient recycling and purification of water will ensure that every drop is maximised. This closed-loop system will be essential for sustaining human life and agriculture, mirroring the water management practices that have been refined on earth. The implementation of these technologies will significantly reduce the strain on resources and allow for the establishment of self-sufficient colonies.

Energy generation systems will play a fundamental role in the sustainability of extraterrestrial habitats. By 2099, it is expected that solar, nuclear, and even fusion energy technologies will be fully operational in off-world environments. The use of solar panels on the surface of planets, combined with nuclear reactors for base load power, will provide a stable energy supply necessary for life-support systems, transportation, and industrial activities. Innovations in energy storage will also be crucial in managing energy availability during periods of low sunlight or high demand, ensuring that colonies can thrive regardless of planetary conditions.

Biodome design and ecosystem management will be key to creating habitable environments. These structures will not only provide shelter from harsh planetary conditions but will also serve as controlled ecosystems for agriculture and recreation. By 2099, biodomes are expected to utilise advanced materials that are both lightweight and durable, capable of withstanding extreme temperatures and radiation. Ecosystem management within these biodomes will involve careful monitoring and adjustment of variables such as humidity, temperature, and atmospheric composition, ensuring a harmonious balance that promotes health and productivity.

Finally, the ethical implications of terraforming and colonising other worlds will necessitate thoughtful policy frameworks. As humanity embarks on this journey, considerations regarding the preservation of any existing extraterrestrial life forms, the environmental impact of human activities, and the rights of future colonists will be paramount. By 2099, it is crucial that international agreements are established to govern these activities, ensuring that the exploration and utilisation of other worlds are conducted responsibly and sustainably. The dialogue surrounding terraforming ethics will shape not only our approach to other planets but also our understanding of our responsibilities as stewards of the cosmos.

Chapter 20: Conclusion and call to action

The importance of terraforming for humanity's future cannot be overstated, especially as earth faces increasing challenges such as climate change, resource depletion, and overpopulation. Terraforming, the process of transforming a planet or moon to create an environment conducive to human life, presents a viable solution to these pressing issues. By the year 2099, advancements in technology and science may enable us to establish habitable worlds beyond our own, providing not just an escape route for humanity, but also a new frontier for exploration and sustainable living. This vision of terraforming encourages innovative thinking and the development of strategies that can help us create self-sustaining ecosystems on other celestial bodies.

One of the key aspects of terraforming is soil enhancement, which is essential for successful extraterrestrial agriculture. The ability to cultivate food in space habitats requires understanding and modifying the soil composition to support crop growth. Techniques such as bioaugmentation and soil microbial inoculation can be applied to create nutrient-rich substrates that mimic earth's fertile soils. By developing robust agricultural systems on other planets, we can ensure food security for off-world colonies, reducing reliance on supplies from earth and promoting a sustainable cycle of production and consumption.

Water sourcing and management stands as another critical component of terraforming efforts. Access to clean water is vital for human survival, agriculture, and maintaining ecosystems. Innovative approaches such as extracting water from subsurface ice, capturing atmospheric moisture, and recycling waste water can be employed to ensure a consistent supply of fresh water. Effective management of these resources will not only support human habitation but also enhance the resilience of the ecosystems we create, allowing for a balanced interaction between different biological and geological processes.

Energy generation systems play a pivotal role in sustaining life on other planets. Harnessing renewable energy sources, such as solar, wind, and geothermal, is essential for powering habitats and supporting various agricultural and industrial activities. The integration of advanced energy storage solutions will also be necessary to ensure a reliable supply during periods of low energy production. By developing these systems, we can create self-sufficient colonies that minimise their environmental impact while maximising efficiency and sustainability, thereby laying the groundwork for long-term human presence in space.

Finally, ethical considerations and policy frameworks surrounding terraforming must be carefully addressed as we venture into creating habitable worlds. The implications of altering extraterrestrial environments raise questions about the rights of potential native life forms, ecological integrity, and our responsibilities as stewards of new worlds. Establishing guidelines that prioritise ecological preservation and respect for any existing ecosystems will be essential for fostering a harmonious relationship with the environments we seek to transform. As we consider the importance of terraforming for humanity's future, it is crucial to balance our ambitions with ethical considerations, ensuring that our quest for survival does not come at the cost of the very worlds we hope to inhabit.

Engaging the public in terraforming initiatives

Engaging the public in terraforming initiatives is essential for the successful adoption and implementation of these transformative projects. As humanity stands on the brink of interplanetary colonisation, public interest and participation can significantly influence funding, policy-making, and technological advancements. By fostering a culture of awareness and enthusiasm around terraforming, we can ensure that initiatives are not only scientifically sound but also socially responsible and widely accepted. One effective way to achieve this is through education and outreach programs that demystify the complexities of terraforming and highlight its potential benefits for humanity.

Public forums and educational workshops can serve as platforms for sharing knowledge about terrestrial terraforming for space habitation by 2099. These events should focus on the practical aspects of soil enhancement methods for extraterrestrial agriculture, illustrating how the science of soil can be adapted to create fertile environments in alien landscapes. By showcasing successful experiments and case studies, we can engage the public's imagination and encourage them to envision a future where sustainable food production is possible beyond earth. Interactive sessions that allow participants to experiment with soil enhancement techniques can further solidify their understanding and interest in these crucial processes.

Water sourcing and management in space habitats is another critical area that can capture public interest. By demonstrating innovative technologies such as atmospheric water generation and recycling systems, we can present solutions to potential challenges that future off-world colonies may face. Engaging the public through demonstrations and virtual reality experiences can provide a tangible sense of how water management will work in extraterrestrial environments. This hands-on approach can help to generate excitement and support for initiatives that aim to secure this vital resource, which is fundamental for human survival in space.

Energy generation systems for sustainable living on other planets must also be a focal point of public engagement. Highlighting advancements in solar, nuclear, and other renewable energy sources can illustrate how these technologies can be adapted for extraterrestrial use. Collaborating with local science centers and educational institutions to create exhibits or competitions related to energy sustainability can inspire the next generation of engineers and scientists. By showcasing the potential for clean energy solutions in off-world colonies, we can not only educate the public but also cultivate a sense of responsibility and ownership regarding the future of space habitation.

Finally, discussions surrounding terraforming ethics and policy frameworks should be integral to public engagement efforts. It is essential to address the moral implications of altering alien ecosystems and the responsibilities humanity bears as it expands beyond earth. By including ethicists, scientists, and community members in dialogues about the ethical dimensions of terraforming, we can create a well-rounded perspective that prioritises respect for potential extraterrestrial environments. Encouraging public discourse on these topics will foster a more informed citizenry, equipped to advocate for responsible and equitable terraforming practices as we move towards the ambitious goal of creating habitable worlds by 2099.

Moving forward: steps to take now

In the journey towards terraforming other planets for human habitation, it is crucial to adopt actionable steps that can guide our efforts effectively. The first step is to prioritise research and development in soil enhancement methods suitable for extraterrestrial environments. Understanding how to create and maintain fertile soil from the raw materials available on other planets is essential for sustainable agriculture. This involves studying soil composition, nutrient delivery systems, and microbial life that can thrive in alien conditions. By investing in innovative agricultural technologies and techniques, we can lay the groundwork for food security in space habitats.

Water sourcing and management are pivotal to establishing viable colonies beyond earth. Developing methods to extract water from ice deposits, which may exist on various celestial bodies, is a critical area of focus. In tandem, efficient recycling systems must be implemented to maximize water use within closed-loop habitats. Advanced filtration and purification technologies can ensure that water remains safe and accessible for consumption and agriculture. Collaborating with experts in hydrology and environmental science will facilitate the creation of sustainable water management strategies tailored to the unique challenges of off-world living.

Energy generation systems will play a vital role in supporting life on other planets. Harnessing renewable energy sources, such as solar and wind, will be fundamental to powering habitats and agricultural systems. Research into nuclear energy as a reliable power source is also necessary, given its potential for long-term sustainability without the limitations of solar dependency during prolonged periods of darkness. Developing energy storage solutions that can withstand harsh extraterrestrial conditions will further enhance the resilience of off-world colonies, ensuring that they can operate independently and efficiently.

The design of biodomes and ecosystem management plans will need serious attention as we prepare for life on other planets. Creating controlled environments that can support diverse ecosystems will require innovative architectural solutions and a deep understanding of ecological dynamics. Utilising local materials for construction, while ensuring the structural integrity of habitats, will be key to minimising resource transport from earth. Additionally, incorporating green technologies (if you can call it that way) and practices into habitat design will foster biodiversity and establish a balanced relationship between human inhabitants and their alien surroundings.

Finally, addressing the ethical implications of terraforming is paramount. Establishing clear policy frameworks will guide the interactions between humans and extraterrestrial environments, ensuring that we do not repeat the mistakes of our own planet. This includes considering the potential impact on any existing ecosystems and the rights of future generations to inherit a habitable world. Furthermore, innovations in health and medical care must be developed to support long-term habitation, addressing the physiological and psychological challenges posed by life in space. By taking these steps now, we can pave the way for successful and responsible terraforming efforts by 2099, ensuring a sustainable future for humanity beyond Earth.

References:

1. The United Nations Office for Outer Space Affairs

(UNOOSA) has been at the forefront of promoting international cooperation in the exploration and use of outer space.

1. The Outer Space Treaty of 1967 serves as the foundation for many international agreements relating to space activities.
2. Books on space travel and exploration
3. Books on planetary science.
4. Books on space administration.

Also by DM Ole Kiminta

How the Western Democracies failed the world
Supporting Refugees in their Homelands
Dissuading Global War Mongers:
Dissuading war mongers
La Libération Monétaire en Afrique
Canada Post: Management failure to modernise mail systems
Canada Post management failure to modernise mail systems
Canada Post: Management failure to modernise mail systems
Live to be 200
Aim to live for 200
Aim to live to be 200
Western democracies failed the world economies
Wrong foot forward: US-Canada trade wars
Canada begs to differ: Never a 51st state of USA
Tethered to the Kitchen
Nous ne pouvons pas être le 51e État des États-Unis
Nous ne serons jamais le 51ème état des États-Unis.
The Nephilim and the erosion of moral boundaries
Every human is an advocate for World Peace
The diplomatic dilemma of Western Sahara
Every human: Advocate for World Peace
The last blue planet

About the Author

DM Ole Kiminta is a Canadian of Maasai heritage. He spent many years working in USA, Britain and in Canada. He is an Industrial engineer, Petroleum engineer and Chemical engineer. Ole Kiminta was educated in USA and United Kingdom. Some of his published research work include Material science, carbon fibres and other composite materials, Polymeric materials, and Particle technology. He currently works for the Canadian government and lives in Toronto Canada with his family.